DATE DUE
DATE DUE
DEC 14 1978

D1017601

*also by Anthony Burgess*

*Fiction*

The Right to an Answer
Devil of a State
A Clockwork Orange
The Wanting Seed
Honey for the Bears
Nothing Like the Sun
The Long Day Wanes
A Vision of Battlements
The Doctor Is Sick
Tremor of Intent
The Eve of Saint Venus
Enderby
MF
One Hand Clapping
Napoleon Symphony

*Nonfiction*

Language Made Plain
Re Joyce
Joysprick
The Novel Now
A Shorter Finnegans Wake
Urgent Copy
Shakespeare

*Translations*

Cyrano de Bergerac
Oedipus the King
The New Aristocrats
The Olive Trees of Justice
The Man Who Robbed Poorboxes

# THE CLOCKWORK TESTAMENT OR ENDERBY'S END

# ANTHONY BURGESS

# THE CLOCKWORK TESTAMENT OR ENDERBY'S END

ILLUSTRATED
BY THE QUAYS

ALFRED A. KNOPF NEW YORK 1975

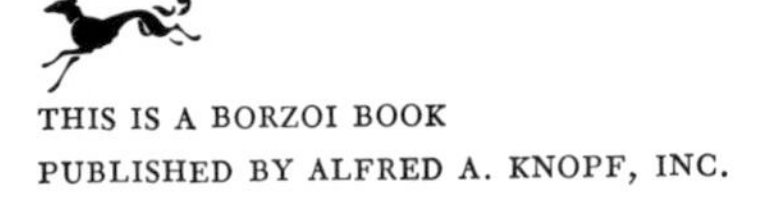

THIS IS A BORZOI BOOK
PUBLISHED BY ALFRED A. KNOPF, INC.

---

 Published in the United States by Alfred A. Knopf, Inc., New York. Distributed by Random House, Inc., New York. Originally published in Great Britain by Hart-Davies, MacGibbon Ltd., London.

LIBRARY OF CONGRESS CATALOGING IN PUBLICATION DATA
Wilson, John Anthony Burgess, (Date)
The clockwork testament.
I. Title.
PZ4.W7492CP3 [PR6073.I4678] 823'.9'14 74-7754
ISBN 0-394-48438-X

*Manufactured in the United States of America*
*First American Edition*

to Burt Lancaster

*". . . deserves to live,*
*deserves to live."*

# THE CLOCKWORK TESTAMENT OR ENDERBY'S END

# ONE

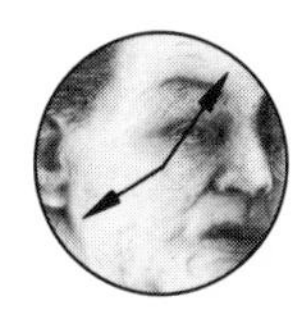

**THE** first thing he saw on waking was his lower denture on the floor, its groove encrusted with dried Dentisement, or it might be Orastik, Mouthficks, Gripdent, or Bite (called *Bait* in Tangier, where he could be said to have a sort of permanent, that is to say, if you could talk of permanency these days in anything, so to speak, address); the fully teethed in my audience will hardly conceive of the variety of denture adhesives on the market. His tongue, at once sprung into life horribly with no prelude of decent morning sluggishness, probed the lower gum briskly and found a diminution of yesterday's soreness. Then it settled into the neutral schwa position to await further directives. So. The denture, incrustations picked loose, laved, recharged with goo of Firmchew—family size with NEW wintergreen flavor—could be jammed in without serious twinge. As well, since today students must be met and talked at.

He lay, naked for the central heating, on his belly. If the bed, which was circular in shape, were a clock, then he was registering twenty of two, as Americans put it, meaning twenty *to* two. If, that was, his upper part were the hour hand. If, that was, twelve o'clock was where the bed touched the wall. The Great Bed of Ware of English legend had been round also, though much bigger, the radius being the length of a sleeper—say six feet. How many pairs of dirty (read Rabelaisian, rollicking) feet meeting at the center(re)? Circumference 2 pi r, was it? It didn't seem big enough somehow. But all the big things of European legend were smaller than you had been brought up to imagine. American scholars sorted that sort of thing out for you. Anybody could eat whole mediaeval sheep, being no bigger than rabbit. Suits of armor(our) would accommodate twelve-year-old American girl. Not enough vitamins in roistering rollicking diet. Hell was originally a rubbish dump outside Jerusalem.

He lay naked also on a fast-drying nocturnal ejaculation, wonderful for man of your age, Enderby. What had the dream been that had conduced to wetness? Being driven in a closed car, muffled to the ears, in black spectacles, funeral sombrero, very pimply guffawing lout driving. Driven into slum street where twelve-year-old girls, Puerto Rican mostly, were playing with a ball. Wait, no, two balls, naturally. The girls jeered, showed themselves knickerless, provoked. He, Enderby, had to go on sitting in black and back of car while guffawing driver got out and ministered very rapidly to them all, their number of course changing all the time. *Finnegans Wake*, ladies and gentlemen, is false to the arithmetic of true dreams, number in that book being an immutable rigidity while, as we know, it is a mutable fluidity in our regular dreaming experience. There are seven biscuits, which you call er cookies, on a plate. You take away, say, two, and three remain. Or, of course, they could be what *you* call biscuits and we, I think, muffins. Principle is the same. I question that, said a sneering Christ of a student. Professor Enderby, asked a what Enderby took to be Polack, Nordic anyway, lacking eyelashes, please clarify your precise threshold of credibility.

This driver lout got through the lot, standing, with quick canine thrusts. Then Enderby was granted discharge and the entire scene, as in some story by that blind Argentinian he had been urged to read by somebody eager and halitotic in the Faculty Lounge, collapsed.

The bed he lay on, twenty of two, squinting down at his watch also on the floor, ten of eight of a New York February morning, was circular because of some philosophy of the regular tenant of the apartment, now on sabbatical and working on Thelma Garstang (1798–1842, bad poetess beaten to death by drunken husband, alleged anyway) in British Museum. The traditional quadrangular bed was male tyranny, or something. This regular tenant was, as well as being an academic, a woman novelist who wrote not very popular novels in which the male characters ended up being castrated. Then, it was implied, or so Enderby understood, not having read any of them, only having been told about them, they became considerate lovers eager for cunnilingus with their castratrices, but they were sneered at for being impotent. Well, he, unimpotent Enderby, temporary professor, would do nothing about cleaning that sperm stain from her circular mattress, ridiculous idea, must have cost a fortune.

Enderby had slept, as now he always did, with his upper denture in. It was a sort of response to the castrating aura of the apartment. He had also found it necessary to be ready for the telephone to ring at all hours, an edentulous chumble getting responses of Pardon me? if the call were a polite one, but if it were insulting or obscene or both, provoking derision. Most of the Serious Calls came from what was known as the Coast and were for his landlady. She was connected with some religiolesbic movement there and she had neglected to send a circular letter about her sabbatical. The insults and obscenities were usually meant for Enderby. He had written a very unwise article for a magazine, in which he said that he thought little of black literature because it tended to tendentiousness and that the Amerindians had shown no evidence of talent for anything except scalping and very inferior folk-craft. One of his callers, who had once termed him a toothless cocksucker (that toothlessness had been right, anyway, at that time anyway), was always threatening to bring a tomahawk to

91st Street and Columbus Avenue, which was where Enderby lodged. Also students would ring anonymously at deliberately awkward hours to revile him for his various faults—chauvinism, or some such thing; ignorance of literary figures important to the young; failure to see merit in their own free verse and gutter vocabulary. They would revile him also in class, of course, but not so freely as on the telephone. Everybody felt naked these days without the mediacy of a mode of mechanical communication.

Eight of eight. The telephone rang. Enderby decided to give it the honour of full dentition, so he jammed in the encrusted lower denture. Try it out. Gum still sorish. But, of course, that was the hardened Gripdent or whatever it was. He had them all.

"Professor Enderby?"

"Speaking."

"You don't know me, but this is just to inform you that both my husband and I consider that your film is filth."

"It's not my film. I only wrote the—"

"You have a lot to answer for, my husband says. Don't you think there's enough juvenile crime in our streets without filth like yours abetting it?"

"But it's not filth and it's not my—"

"Obscene filth. Let me inform you that my husband is six feet three and broad in proportion—"

"Is he a red Indian?"

"That's just the sort of cheap insult I would expect from a man capable of—"

"If you're going to send him round here, with or without tomahawk—"

She had put down the receiver. What he had been going to say was that there was twenty-four-hour armed protection in the apartment lobby as well as many closed-circuit television screens. This, however, would not help him if the enemies were within the block itself. That he had enemies in the block he knew—a gat-toothed black writer and his wife; a single woman with dogs who had objected to his mentioning in his magazine article the abundance of cockroaches in this part of Manhattan, as though it were a shameful family secret; a couple of fattish electronic guitarists who had smelt his loathing as they had gone up together once in the elevator. And there might be also others affronted by the film just this moment referred to.

Flashback. Into the bar-restaurant Enderby, exiled poet, ran in Tangier, film men had one day come. Kasbah location work or something of the kind. One of the film men, who had seemed and indeed proved to be big in his field, an American director considered for the brilliance of his visual invention quite as good as any director in Europe, said something about wanting to make, because of the visual possibilities, a shipwreck film. Enderby, behind bar and hence free to join in conversation without any imputation of insolence, having also British accent, said something about *The Wreck of the Deutschland.*

"Too many Kraut Kaput movies lately. Last days of Hitler, Joe Krankenhaus already working on Goebbels, then there was Visconti."

"A ship," said Enderby, "called the *Deutschland.* Hopkins wrote it."

"Al Hopkins?"

"G.M.," Enderby said, adding, "S.J."

"Never heard of him. Why does he want all those initials?"

"Five Franciscan nuns," Enderby said, "exiled from Germany because of the Falk Laws. 'On Saturday sailed from Bremen, American-outward-bound, take settler and seaman, tell men with women, two hundred souls in the round . . .' "

"He knows it all, by God. When?"

"1875. December 7th."

"Nuns," mused the famed director. "What were these laws?"

" 'Rhine refused them. Thames would ruin them,' " Enderby said. " 'Surf, snow, river and earth,' " he said, " 'gnashed.' "

"Totalitarian intolerance," the director's assistant and friend said. "Nuns beaten up in the streets. Habits torn off. Best done in flashback. The storm symbolic as well as real. What happens at the end?" he asked keenly Enderby.

"They all get wrecked in the Goodwin Sands. The Kentish Knock, to be precise. And then there's this final prayer. 'Let him easter in us, be a dayspring to the dimness of us, be a crimson-cresseted east . . .' "

"In movies," the director said kindly, as to a child, "you don't want too many words. You see that? It's what we call a visual medium. Two more double scatches on the racks."

"I know all about that," Enderby said with heat, pouring whisky sightlessly for these two men. "When they did my *Pet Beast* it became nothing but visual clichés. In Rome it was. Cinecittà. The bastard. But he's dead now."

"Who's dead?"

"Rawcliffe," Enderby said. "He used to own this place." The two men stared at him. "What I mean is," Enderby said, "that there was this film. Movie, you'd call it, ridiculous word. In Italian, *L'Animal Binato*. That was *Son of the Beast from Outer Space*. In English that is," he explained.

"But that," the director said, "was a small masterpiece. Alberto Formica, dead now poor bastard, well ahead of his time. The clichés were deliberate, it summed up a whole era. So." He looked at Enderby with new interest. "What did you say your name was? Rawcliffe? I always thought Rawcliffe was dead."

"Enderby," Enderby said. "Enderby the poet."

"You did the script, you say?" the assistant and friend said.

"I wrote *The Pet Beast*."

"Why," the director said, taking out a visiting card from among embossed instruments of international credit, "don't you write us a letter, the shipwreck story I mean, setting it all out?"

Enderby smiled knowingly, a poet but up to their little tricks. "I give you a film script for nothing," he said. "I've heard of this letter business before." The card read *Melvin Schaumwein, Chisel Productions*. "If I do you a script I shall want paying for it."

"How much?" said Mr. Schaumwein.

Enderby smiled. "A lot," he said. The money part of his brain grew suddenly delirious, lifelong abstainer fed with sudden gin. He trembled as with the prospect of sexual outrage. "A thousand dollars," he said. They stared at him. "There," he said. And then: "Somewhere in that region anyway. I'm not what you'd call a greedy man."

"We might manage five hundred," Schaumwein's assistant-friend said. "On delivery, of course. Provided that it's what might be termed satisfactory."

"Seven hundred and fifty," Enderby said. "I'm not what you'd call a greedy man."

"It's not an original," Mr. Schaumwein said. "You mentioned some guy called Hopkins that wrote the book. Who is he, where is he, who do I see about the rights?"

"Hopkins," Enderby said, "died in 1889. His poems were published in 1918. *The Wreck of the Deutschland* is out of copyright."

"I think," Mr. Schaumwein said carefully, "we'll have two more scatches on the racks."

What, after Mr. Schaumwein had gone back to the Kasbah and then presumably home to Chisel Productions, was to surprise Enderby was that the project was to be taken seriously presumably. For a letter came from the friend-assistant, name revealed as Martin Droeshout (familiar vaguely to Enderby in some vague picture connection or other), confirming that, for $750.00, Enderby would deliver a treatment for a film tentatively entitled *The Wreck of the Deutschland*, based on a story by Hopkins, which story their researchers had not been able to bring to light despite prolonged research, had Enderby got the name right, but it didn't matter as subject was in public domain. Enderby presumed that the word *treatment* was another word for *shooting script* (a lot of film men had been to his bar at one time or another, so the latter term was familiar to him). He had even looked at the shooting script of a film in which a heavy though not explicit sexual sequence had actually been shot, at midnight with spotlights and a humming generator truck, on the beach just near to his beach café-restaurant, La Belle Mer. So, while his boys snored or writhed sexually with each other during the siesta, he got down to typewriter-pecking out his cinematisation of a great poem, delighting in such curt visual directives as VLS, CU, and so on, though not always clearly understanding what they meant.

1. EXTERIOR NIGHT
*Lightning lashes a rod on top of a church.*

PRIEST'S VOICE: Yes. Yes. Yes.

2. INTERIOR NIGHT A CHURCH
*Thunder rolls. A priest on his knees at the altar looks up, sweating. It is Fr. Hopkins, S.J.*

FR. HOPKINS, S.J.: Thou heardest me truer than tongue confess Thy terror, O Christ, O God.

3. EXTERIOR NIGHT A STARLIT SKY
*The camera pans slowly across lovely-asunder starlight.*

4. EXTERIOR NIGHT THE GROUNDS OF A THEOLOGICAL SEMINARY
*Father Hopkins, S.J., looks up ecstatically at all the firefolk sitting in the air and then kisses his hand at them.*

5. EXTERIOR SUNSET THE DAPPLED-WITH-DAMSON WEST
*Father Hopkins, S.J., kisses his hand at it.*

6. INTERIOR DAY A REFECTORY
*The scene begins with a* CU *of Irish stew being placed on a table by an ill-girt scullion. Then the camera pulls back to show priests talking vigorously.*

PRIEST #1: These Falk Laws in Germany are abominable and totally sinful.

PRIEST #2: I hear that a group of Franciscan nuns are sailing to America next Saturday.

*The voice of Father Hopkins, S.J., is heard from another part of the table.*

HOPKINS (OS): Glory be to God for dappled things—
For skies of couple-colour as a brinded cow . . .

*The priests look at each other.*

7. THE SAME TWO SHOT
*Father Hopkins is talking earnestly to a very beautiful fellow-priest, who listens attentively.*

HOPKINS: Since, though he is under the world's splendour and wonder, his mystery must be instressed, stressed . . .

FELLOW-PRIEST: I quite understand.

*The camera pans rapidly back to the other two priests, who look at each other.*

PRIEST #1:
(*sotto voce*)
Jesus Christ.

It worried Enderby a little, as he proceeded with his film version of the first part of the poem, that Hopkins should appear to be a bit cracked. There was also a problem in forcing a relevance between the first part and the second. Enderby, serving one morning abstractedly sloe gin to two customers, hit on a solution. "Sacrifice," he said suddenly. The customers took their sloe gins away to a far table. The idea being that Hopkins wanted to be Christ but that the tall nun, Gertrude, kindly became Christ for him, and that her sort of crucifixion on the Kentish Knock (sounded, he thought gloomily, like some rural sexual aberration) might conceivably be thought of as helping to bring our King back, oh, upon English souls.

12. EXTERIOR DAY CU A SLOE
*We see a lush-kept plush-capped sloe in a white well-kept priestly hand.*

13. CU FATHER HOPKINS, S.J.
*Hopkins, in very large close-up, mouths the sloe to flesh-burst. He shudders.*

14. EXTERIOR DAY CALVARY
*Christ is being nailed to the cross. Roman soldiers jeer.*

15. RESUME 13.
*Hopkins, still shuddering, looks down at the bitten sloe. The camera tracks on to it into* CU. *It dissolves into:*

16. INTERIOR DAY A CHURCH
*The hands of a priest hold up the host, which looks a bit like the sloe. It is, of course, Fr. Hopkins, S.J., saying mass.*

17. THE SAME CU
*In* CU, *Father Hopkins murmurs ecstatically.*

HOPKINS:
(*ecstatically*)
Be adored among men, God, three-numberèd form. Wring thy rebel, dogged in den, man's malice, with wrecking and storm.

18. EXTERIOR DAY A STORMY SEA
*The* Deutschland, *American-outward-bound. Death on drum, and storms bugle his fame.*

The second part was easier, mostly a business of copying out Hopkins' own what might be thought of as prophetic camera directions:

45. EXTERIOR DAY THE SEA
*Wiry and white-fiery and whirlwind-swivellèd snow spins to the widow-making unchilding unfathering deeps.*

And so on. When it was finished it made, Enderby thought, a very nice little script. It could be seen also as the tribute of one poet to another. People would see the film and then go and read the poem. They would see the poem as superior art to the film. He sent the script off to Mr. Schaumwein at Chisel Productions. He eventually received a brief letter from Martin Droeshout saying that a lot of it was very flowery, but that was put down to Enderby's being a poet, which claim of Enderby had been substantiated by researchers. However, they were going ahead, updating so as to make Germany Nazi, and making the nun Gertrude a former love of Father

Hopkins, both of them coming to realisation that it was God they really loved but they would keep in touch. This meant rewrite men, as Enderby would realise, but Enderby's name would appear among the credits.

Enderby's name did indeed eventually appear among the credits: *Developed out of an idea of.* Also he was invited to London to see a preview of *The Wreck of the Deutschland* (they couldn't think of a better title, any of them; there wasn't a better title). He was pretty shocked by a lot of it, especially the flashbacks, and it was nearly all flashbacks, the only present-tense reality being the *Deutschland* on its way to be ground to bits on the Kentish Knock (which, somebody else at the preview said, to ecstatic laughter, sounded a little like a rural sexual aberration). For instance, Hopkins, who had been given quite arbitrarily the new name Tom, eventually Father Tom, was Irish, and the tall nun was played by a Swede, though that was really all right. These two had a great pink sexual encounter, but before either of them took vows, so that, Enderby supposed, was all right too. There were some overexplicit scenes of the nuns being violated by teen-age storm troopers. The tall nun Gertrude herself tore off her Franciscan habit to make bandages during the storm scenes, so that her end, in a posture of crucifixion on the Kentish Knock, was as near nude as that of her Master. There was also an ambiguous moment when, storms bugling, though somewhat subdued, Death's fame in the background, she cried orgasmatically: "Oh Christ, Christ, come quickly"—Hopkins' own words, so one could hardly complain. On the whole, not a bad film, with Hopkins getting two seconds worth of solo credit: *Based on the poem by.* As was to be expected, it got a very restrictive showing rating, nobody under eighteen. "Things have come to a pretty pass," said Mr. Schaumwein in a television interview, "when a religious film is no longer regarded as good family viewing."

So there it was then, except for complaints from the reactionary and puritanical, though not, as far as Enderby could tell, from Hopkins' fellow-Jesuits. *The Month,* which had originally refused the poem itself, made amends by finding the film adult and serious. "Mr. Schaumwein very sensibly has eschewed the temptation to translate Hopkins' confused grammar and neologistic tortuosities into corresponding visual obscurities." Enderby's association, however small, with a great demotic medium led to his being considered worthy by the University of Manhattan of being invited to come as a visiting professor for an academic year. The man who sent the invitation, the Chairman of the English Department, Alvin Kosciusko, said that Enderby's poems were not unknown there in the United States. Whatever anybody thought of them, there was no doubt that they were genuine Creative Writing. Enderby was therefore cordially invited to come and pass on some of his Creative Writing skill to Creative Writing students. His penchant for old-fashioned and traditional forms might act as a useful corrective to the cult of free form, which, though still rightly flourishing, had led to some excesses. One postgraduate student had received a prize for a poem that turned out to be a passage from a vice-presidential speech copied out in reverse and then seasoned with mandatory obscenities. He had protested that it was as much Creative Writing as any of the shit that had been awarded prizes in previous years. Anyway, the whole business of giving prizes was reactionary. Subsidies were what was required.

# TWO

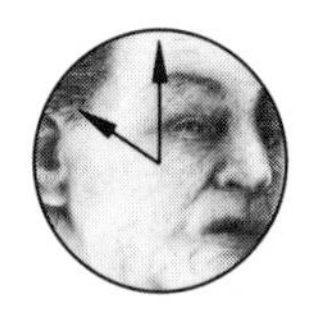

**NAKED** as the day he was born though much hairier, Enderby prepared himself breakfast. One of the things he approved of about New York—a city otherwise dirty, rude, violent, and full of foreigners and mad people—was the wide variety of dyspeptic foods on sale in the supermarkets. In his view, if you did not get dyspepsia while or after eating, you had been cheated of essential nourishment. As for dealing with the dyspepsia, he had never in his life seen so many palliatives for it available—Stums and Windkill and Eupep and (magnificent proleptic onomatopoesis, the work of some high-paid Madison Avenue genius, sincerely admired by Enderby) Aaaarp. And so on. But the best of all he had discovered in a small shop specialising in Oriental medicines (sent thither by a Chinese waiter)—a powerful black viscidity that oozed sinisterly from a tube to bring wind up from Tartarean depths. When he went to buy it, the shopkeeper would, in his earthy Chinese manner, designate it with a remarkable phonic mime of the substance at work. Better than Aaaarp but not easily representable in any conventional alphabet. Enderby would nod kindly, pay, take, bid good day, go.

Enderby had become, so far as use of the culinary resources of the kitchen (at night the cockroaches' playground) were concerned, one hundred per cent Americanised. He would whip up a thick milk shake in the mixer, thaw then burn frozen waffles in the toaster, make soggy leopardine pancakes with Aunt Jemima's buckwheat pancake mixture (Aunt Jemima herself was on the packet, a comely Negress rejoicing in her bandanna'd servitude), fry Oscar Mayer fat little sausages. His nakedness would be fat-splashed, but the fat easily washed off, unlike with clothes. And he would make tea, though not altogether in the American manner—five bags in a pint mug with ALABAMA gilded onto it, boiling water, a long stewing, very sweet condensed milk added. He would eat his breakfast with H.P. steak sauce on one side of the plate, maple syrup on the other. The Americans went in for synchronic sweet and savoury, a sign of their salvation, unlike the timid Latin races. He would end his meal with a healthy slice of Sara Lee orange cream cake, drink another pint of tea, then, after his black Chinese draught, be alertly ready for work. A man-sized breakfast, as they said. There was never need for much lunch—some canned corned-beef hash with a couple of fried eggs, say, and a pint of tea. A slice of banana cake. And then, this being America, a cup of coffee.

Heartburn was slow in coming this morning, which made Enderby, stickler for routine, uneasy. He noted also with rueful pride that, despite the emission of the night, he was bearing before him as he left the kitchen, where he had eaten as well as cooked, a sizeable horizontal ithyphallus lazily swinging towards the vertical. Something to do perhaps with excessive protein intake. He took it to a dirty towel in the bathroom, called those Puerto Rican bitches back from that dream, then gave it them all. The street was littered with them. The pimpled lout, astonished and fearful, ran round the corner. This meant that Enderby would have to drive the car away himself. He at once sold it for a trifling sum to a grey-haired black man who shuffled out of an open doorway, evening newspaper in his hand, and made his get-away, naked, on foot. Then dyspepsia struck, he took his black drops, released a savoury gale from as far down as the very caecum, and was ready for work, his own work, not the pseudo-work he would have to do in the afternoon with pseudo-students. For that he must shave, dress, wash, probably in that order. Take the subway, as they called it. Brave mean streets full of black and brown menace.

Enderby, still naked, sat at his landlady's desk in the bedroom. It was a small apartment, there was no study. He supposed he was lucky to have gotten (very American touch there: *gotten*) an apartment at all at the rent he was able, the salary not being overlarge, to pay. His landlady, a rabid ideological man-hater, had addressed one letter to him from her digs in Bayswater, confirming that he pay the black woman Priscilla to come and clean for him every Saturday, thus maintaining a continuity of her services useful for when his landlady should return to New York. Enderby was not sure what sex she thought he, Enderby, had, since there was a reference to not trying to flush sanitary pads down the toilet. The title *professor*, which she rightly addressed him by, was common, as the old grammars would put it. Perhaps she had read his poems and found a rich femininity in them; perhaps some kind man in the English Department had represented Enderby as an ageing but progressive spinster to her when she sought to let her apartment. Anyway, he had answered the letter promptly on his own portable typewriter, signing with a delicate hand, assuring her that sanitary pads would go out with the garbage and that Priscilla was being promptly paid and not overworked (lazy black insolent bitch, thought Enderby, but evidently illiterate and not likely to blow the sex gaff in letter or transatlantic cable). So there it was. On the other hand, his landlady might learn in London from librarians or in communications from members of the Californian religiolesbic sorority that Enderby was really a (*sounded suspiciously like the voice of an MCP to me, toothless too, a TMCP, what little game are you playing, dear?*). But it was probably too late for her to do anything about it now. Couldn't evict him on grounds of his sex. The United

Nations, conveniently here in New York, would, through an appropriate department, have something very sharp to say about that. So there it was, then. Enderby got down to work.

Back in Morocco, as previously in England, Enderby was used to working in the toilet, piling up drafts and even fair copies in the never-used bath. Here it would not do, since the bath taps dripped and the toilet seat was (probably by some previous Jewish-mother tenant who wished to discourage solitary pleasures among her menfolk) subtly notched. It was ungrateful to the bottom. Neither was there a writing table low enough. Nor would Priscilla understand. This eccentric country was great on conformity. Enderby now wrote at the desk that had produced so many androphobic mistresspieces. What he was writing was a long poem about St. Augustine and Pelagius, trying to sort out for himself and a couple of score readers the whole worrying business of predestination and free will. He read through what he had so far written, scratching and grunting, naked, a horrible White Owl cigar in his mouth.

*He came out of the misty island, Morgan,*
*Man of the sea, demure in monk's sackcloth,*
*Taking the long way to Rome, expecting—*
*Expecting what? Oh, holiness quintessentialised,*
*Holiness whole, the wholesome wholemeal of,*
*Holiness as meat and drink and air, in the*
*Chaste thrusts of marital love holiness, and*
*Sanctitas sanctitas even snaking up from*
*Cloacae and sewers, sanctitas the effluvium*
*From His Holiness's arsehole.*

Perhaps that was going a bit too far. Enderby poised a ballpoint, dove, retracted. No, it was the right touch really. Let the *arsehole* stay. Americans preferred *asshole* for some reason. This then very British. But why not? Pelagius was British. Keep *arsehole* in.

*On the long road*
*Trudging, dust, birdsong, dirty villages,*
*Stops on the way at monasteries (weeviled bread,*
*Eisel wine), always this thought:* Sanctitas.
*What dost seek in Rome, brother? The home*
*Of holiness, to lodge awhile in the*
*Sanctuary of sanctity, my brothers, for here*
*Peter died, seeing before he died*
*The pagan world inverted to sanctitas, and*
*The very flagged soil is rich with the bonemeal*
*Of the martyrs. And the brothers would*
*Look at each other, each thinking, some saying:*
*Here cometh one that only islands breed.*
*What can flourish in that Ultima Thule save*
*Holiness, a bare garment for the wind to*
*Sing through? And not Favonius either but*
*Sour Boreas from the pole. Not the grape,*
*Not garlic not the olive, not the strong sun*
*Tickling the manhood in a man, be he*
*Monk or friar or dean or*
*Burly bishop, big ballocks swinging like twin censers.*
*Only holiness. God help him, God bless him for*
*We look upon British innocence.*
*And the British innocent, hurtful of no man,*
*Fond of dogs, a cat-stroker,*
*Trudged on south—vine, olive, garlic,*
*Brown tits jogging while brown feet*
*Danced in the grapepress and the*
*Baaark ballifoll goristafick*

That last was inner Enderby demanding the stool. He took his poem with him thither, frowning, sat reading.

*Monstrous aphrodisiac danced in the heavens*
*Prrrrrrp faaaark*
*Wheep*
*Till at length he came to the outer suburbs and*
*Fell on his knees* O sancta urbs sancta sancta
*Meaning sancta suburbs and*
*Plomp*

Enderby wiped himself with slow care and marched back, frowning, reading. As he reached the telephone on the bed table the telephone rang, so that he was able to pick it up at once, thus disconcerting the voice on the other end, which had not expected such promptitude.

"Oh. Mr. Enderby?" It was a woman's voice, being higher than a man's. American female voices lacked feminine timbre as known in the south of vine and garlic, were just higher because of accident of larynx being smaller.

"Professor Enderby speaking."

"Oh, hi. This is the Sperr Lansing Show. We wondered if you—"

"What? Who? What is this?"

"The Sperr Lansing Show. A talk show. Television. *The* talk show. Channel Fif—"

"Ah, I see," Enderby said, with British heartiness. "I've seen it, I think. She left it here, you see. Extra on the rent."

"Who? What?"

"Oh, I see what you mean. Yes. A television. She's a great one for her rights. Ah yes, I've seen it a few times. A sort of thin man with a fat jackal. Both leer a good deal, but one supposes they have to."

"No, no, you have the wrong show there, professor." The title now seemed pretentious, also absurd, as when someone in a film is addressed as *professor*. "What you mean is the Cannon Dickson Show. That's mostly show-business personalities. The Sperr Lansing Show is, well, *different*."

"I didn't really mean to insist, ha ha," Enderby said, "on the title of professor. Fancy dress, you know. A lot of nonsense really. And I really must apologise for—" He was going to say *for being naked:* it was all this damned visual stuff. "For my innocence. I mean my ignorance."

"I guess I ought to introduce myself, as we've already been talking for such a long time. I'm Midge Tauchnitz."

"Enderby," Enderby said. "Sorry, that was— So, eh? 'The strong spur, live and lancing like the blowpipe flame.' I suppose that's where he got it from."

"Pardon me?"

"Anyway, thank you for calling."

"No, it doesn't go out live. Nothing these days goes out live."

"I promise to watch it at the earliest opportunity. Thank you very much for suggesting—"

"No, no, we want you to appear on it. We record at seven, so you'd have to be here about six."

"Why?" Enderby said in honest surprise. "For God's sake why?"

"Oh, make-up and so on. It's on West 46th Street, between Fifth and—"

"No, no, no. Why me?"

"Pardon me?"

"Me."

"Oh." The voice became teasing and girlish. "Oh, come now, professor, that's playing it too cool. It's the movie. *The Deutschland*."

"Ah. But I only wrote the— I mean, it was only my idea. That's what it says, anyway. Why don't you ask one of the others, the ones who really made it?"

"Well," she said candidly. "We tried to get hold of Bob Ponte, the script writer, but he's in Honolulu writing a script, and Mr. Schaumwein is in Rome, and Millennium suggested we get on to you. So I phoned the university and they gave us your—"

"Hopkins," Enderby said, in gloomy play. "Did you try Hopkins?"

"No luck there either. Nobody knows where he is."

"In the eschatological sense, I should think it's pretty certain that—"

"Pardon me?"

"But in the other it's no wonder. 1844 to 89," he twinkled.

"Oh, I'll write that down. But it doesn't sound like a New York number—"

"No no no no no. A little joke. He's dead, you see."

"Gee, I'm sorry, I didn't know. But you're okay? I mean, you'll be there?"

"If you really want me. But I still don't see—"

"You don't? You don't read the newspapers?"

"Never. And again never. A load of frivolity and lies. They've been attacking it, have they?"

"No. Some boys have been attacking some nuns. In Manhattanville. I'm shocked you didn't know. I assumed—"

"Nuns are always being attacked. Their purity is an affront to the dirty world."

"Remember that. Remember to say that. But the point is that they said they wouldn't have done it if they hadn't seen the movie. That's why we're—"

"I see. I see. Always blame art, eh? Not original sin but art. I'll have my say, never fear."

"You have the address?"

"You ignore art as so much unnecessary garbage or you blame it for your own crimes. That's the way of it. I'll get the bastards, all of them. I'm not having this sort of nonsense, do you hear?" There was silence at the other end. "You never take art for what it is—beauty, ultimate meaning, form for its own sake, self-subsisting, oh no. It's always got to be either sneered at or attacked as evil. I'll have my bloody say. What's the name of the show again?" But she had rung off, silly bitch.

Enderby went snorting back to his poem. The stupid bastards.

*But wherever he went in Rome, it was always the*
*same—*
*Sin sin sin, no sanctity, the whole unholy*
*Grammar of sin, syntax, accidence, sin's*
*Entire lexicon set before him, sin.*
*Peacocks in the streets, gold dribbled over*
*In dark rooms, vomiting after*
*Banquets of ostrich bowels stuffed with saffron,*
*Minced pikeflesh and pounded larkbrain,*
*Served with a sauce headily fetid, and pocula*
*Of wine mixed with adder's blood to promote*
*Lust lust and again.*
*Pederasty, podorasty, sodomy, bestiality,*
*Degrees of family ripped apart like*
*Bodices in the unholy dance. And he said,*
*And Morgan said, whom the scholarly called*
*Pelagius:*
*Why do ye this, my brothers and sisters?*
*Are ye not saved by Christ, are ye not*
*Sanctified by his sacrifice, oh why why why?*
*(Being British and innocent) and*

What was the name of that show again? Art blamed as always. Art was neutral, neither teaching nor provoking, a static shimmer, he would tell the bastards. What was it again? And then he thought about this present poem (a draft of course, very much a draft) and wondered: *is it perhaps not didactic?* But how about *The Wreck of the Deutschland?* Hopkins was always having a go at the English, and the Welsh too, for not rushing to be converted back (the marvellous milk was Walsingham Way, once) to Catholicism. But somehow Hopkins was of the devil's party without knowing it (better remember not to say that on this Live Lancing Show, that was the name, something like it anyway, people were stupid, picked you up literally on that sort of thing): it was a kind of paganism with him—lush-kept plush-capped sloe, indeed—with God tacked on. The our-King-back-oh-upon-English-souls stuff was merely structural, something to bring the poem to an end. But how about this?

No, he decided. He was not preaching. Who the hell was he to preach? Out of the Church at sixteen, never been to mass in forty years. This was merely an imaginative inquiry into free will and predestination. Somewhat comforted, he read on, scratching, the White Owl, self-doused, relighted, hooting out foul smoke.

*They said to him cheerfully, looking up*
*From picking a peahen bone or kissing the*
*Nipple or nates of son, daughter, sister,*
*Brother, aunt, ewe, teg: Why, stranger,*
*Hast not heard the good news? That Christ*
*Took away the burden of our sins on his*
*Back broad to bear, and as we are saved*
*Through him it matters little what we do?*
*Since we are saved once for all, our being*

*Saved will not be impaired or cancelled by*
*Our present pleasures (which we propose to*
*Renew tomorrow after a suitable and well-needed*
*Rest). Alleluia alleluia to the Lord for he has*
*Led us to two paradises, one to come and the other*
*Here and now. Alleluia. And they fell to again,*
*To nipple or nates or fish baked with datemince,*
*Alleluia. And Morgan cried to the sky:*
*How long O Lord wilt thou permit these*
*Transgressions against thy holiness?*
*Strike them strike them as thou once didst*
*The salty cities of the plain, as through*
*Phinehas the son of Eleazar the son of Aaron*
*Thou didst strike down the traitor Zimri*
*And his foul whore of the Moabite temples Cozbi.*
*Strike strike. But the Lord did nothing.*

Here came the difficulties. This whole business of free will and predestination and original sin had to be done very dramatically. And yet there had to be a bit of sermonising. How the hell? Enderby, who was not at present wearing his spectacles (ridiculous when one was otherwise naked, anyway he only needed them for distance really), gazing vaguely about the bedroom for an answer found none forthcoming. The bookshelves of his landlady sternly turned the backs, spines rather, of their contents towards him: not our business, we are concerned with the *real* issues of life, meaning women downtrodden by men, the economic oppression of the blacks, counter-culture, coming revolt, Reich, Fanon, third world. Then Enderby, squinting, could hardly believe what he saw. At the bedroom door a woman, girl, female anyway. Covering his genitals with his poem he said:

"What the devil? Who let you? Get out."

"But I have an appointment with you at ten. It's ten after now. It was arranged. I'll wait in the— Unless— I mean, I didn't expect—"

She had not yet gone. Enderby, pumping strongly at the White Owl as if it would thus make him an enveloping cloud, turned his back to her, covered his bottom with his poem, then found his dressing gown (Rawcliffe's really, bequeathed to him with his other effects) on a chair behind a rattan settee and near to the air conditioner. He clothed himself in it. She was still there and talking.

"I mean, I don't mind if you don't—"

"I do mind," Enderby said. And he flapped towards her on bare feet but in his gown. "What is all this anyway?"

"For *Jesus.*"

"For *who*, for Christ's sake?" He was close to her now and saw that she was a nice little thing he supposed she could be called, with nicely sculpted little tits under a black sweater stained with, as he supposed, Coke and Pepsi and hamburger fat (*good food* was what these poor kids needed), long American legs in patched worker's pants. Strange how one never bothered to take in the face here in America, the face didn't matter except on films, one never remembered the face, and all the voices were the same. And then: "They shouldn't have let you in, you know, just like that. You're supposed to be screened or something, and then they ring me up and ask if it's all right."

"But he knows me, the man downstairs. He knows I'm one of your students."

"Oh, are you?" said Enderby. "I didn't quite— Yes," peering at her, "I suppose you could be. We'd better go into the sitting room or whatever they call it." And he pushed past her into the corridor to lead the way.

The room where he was supposed to *live* (e.g., watch television, play protest songs on his landlady's record player, look out of the window down on the street at acts of violence) was furnished mostly with barbaric nonsense—drums and shields and spears and very ill-woven garish rugs—and you were supposed to sit on *pouffes*. Enderby waved this girl to a *pouffe* with one hand and with the other indicated the television set, saying, puffing out White Owl smoke, "I'm to be on that thing there."

"Oh."

"The Blowpipe Show or something. Can't think of the name offhand. What did you say your name was?"

"Oh, you *know*. Lydia Tietjens." And, as he sat on a neighbouring *pouffe*, she gave him a playful push, as at his rather nice eccentric foreign silliness.

"Ah yes, of course. Ford Madox Ford. Met him once. He had terrible halitosis, you know. Stood in his way. The Establishment rejected him. And it was because he'd had the guts to fight and get gassed, while the rest of the bastards stayed at home. I say, you're not recording that, are you?" For, he now saw, she had a small Japanese cassette machine and was holding it towards him, rather like a sideswoman with offertory box.

"Just getting a level." And then, after some whirring and clicking, Enderby heard an unfamiliar voice say: *rest of the bastards stayed at home i say youre not rec.*

"What did you say it was for?"

"For *Jesus*. Our magazine. Women for Jesus. *You know*."

"Why just women for Jesus? I thought anyone could join." And Enderby looked with fascination at the Xeroxed thing she brought out of what looked like a British respirator haversack—*their* magazine, typewritten, as he could see from the last page, with no margin justifying, and the front page just showing the name JESUS and a crude portrait of a beardless though plentifully haired messiah.

"But that's not him."

"Right. Not *him*. What proof is there that it was a *him?*"

Enderby breathed hard a few times and said: "Would you like what we English call elevenses? Cakes and tea and things? I could cook you a steak if you liked. Or, wait, I have some stew left over from yesterday. It wouldn't take a minute to heat it up." That was the trouble with all of them, poor kids. Half-starved, seeing visions, poisoned with Cokes and hamburgers.

# THREE

**DO** you believe in God?" she asked, a steak sandwich in one paw and the cassette thing in the other.

"Is that tea strong enough for you?" Enderby asked. "It doesn't look potable to me. One bag indeed. Gnat piss," he added. And then: "Oh, God. Well, believing is neither here nor there, you know. I believe in God and so what? I don't believe in God and so what again? It doesn't affect his own position, does it?"

"Why do you say *his?*" she hizzed.

"Her, then. It. Doesn't matter really. A matter of tradition and convention and so on. Needs a new pronoun. Let's invent one, unique, just for—himherit. Ah, that's it, then. Nominative *heshit*. Accusative *himrit*. Genitive *hiserits*."

"But you're still putting the masculine first. The *heshit* bit's all right, though. Appropriate."

"I don't mind what goes first," Enderby said. "Would you like something by Sara Lee? Please yourself then. All right. *Shehit. Herimit. Herisits.* It doesn't affect herisits position whether I believe or not."

"But what happens when you die?"

"You're finished with," Enderby said promptly. "Done for. And even if you weren't—well, you die then, gasp your last, then you're sort of wandering, free of your body. You wander around and then you come into contact with a sort of big thing. What is this big thing? God, if you like. What's it, or shehit, like? I would say," Enderby said thoughtfully, "like a big symphony, the page of the score of infinite length, the number of instruments infinite but all bound into one big unity. This big symphony plays itself for ever and ever. And who listens to it? It listens to itself. Enjoys itself for ever and ever and ever. It doesn't give a bugger whether you hear it or not."

"Like masturbation."

"I thought it would come to that. I thought you'd have to bring sex into it sooner or later. Anyway, a kind of infinite Ninth Symphony. God as Eternal Beauty. God as Truth? Nonsense. God as Goodness. That means shehit has to be in some sort of ethical relationship with beings that are notGod. But God is removed, cut off, self-subsistent, not giving a damn."

"But that's horrible. I couldn't live with a God like that."

"You don't have to. Anyway, what have you or anybody else got to do with it? God doesn't have to be what people want shehit to be. I'm fed up with God," Enderby said, "so let's get on to something else." And at once he got up painfully and noisily to find the whisky bottle, this being about the time for. "I haven't got any glasses," he said. "Not clean ones, anyway. You'll have to have it from the bottle."

"I don't want any." She didn't want her tea either. Quite right: gnat piss. Enderby got down again. "If there's no life after death," she said, "why does it matter about doing good in this world? I mean, if there's no reward or punishment in the next."

"That's terrible," Enderby sneered. "Doing things because of what you're bloody well going to get out of it." He took some whisky and did a conventional shudder. It raged briefly through the inner streets and then was transmuted into benevolent warmth in the citadel. Enderby smiled on the girl kindly and offered the bottle. She took it, raised it like a trumpet to the heavens, sucked in a millilitre or so. "And, while we're at it," he said, "let's decide what we mean by good."

"You decide. It's you who are being interviewed."

"Well, there are some stupid bastards who can't understand how the commandant of a Nazi concentration camp could go home after torturing Jews all day and then weep tears of joy at a Schubert symphony on the radio. They say: here's a man dedicated to evil capable of enjoying the good. But what the imbecilic sods don't realise is that there are two kinds of good—one is neutral, outside ethics, purely aesthetic. You get it in music or in a sunset if you like that sort of thing or in a grilled steak or in an apple. If God's good, if God exists that is, God's probably good in that way. As I said." He sipped from the bottle she had handed back. "Before."

"Or sex. Sex is as good whether— I mean, you don't have to be in what they used to call a state of grace to enjoy it."

"That's good," Enderby said warmly. "That's right. Though you're still going on about sex. You mean lesbian sex, of course, in your case. Not that I have anything against it, naturally, except that I'm not permitted to experience it. The world's getting narrower all the time. All little sects doing what they call their own thing."

"Why do you keep showing your balls all the time?" she said boldly. "Don't you have underpants or anything?"

Enderby flushed very deeply all over. "I had no intention," he said. "I can assure you. What I mean is, I'll put something on. I was not trying to provoke— I apologise," he said, going off back to the bedroom. He came out again wearing nondescript trousers, something from an old suit, and a not overclean striped shirt. Also slippers. He said, "There." The hypocritical little bitch had been at the bottle in his brief absence. He could tell that from her slight slur. She said:

"Evil."

"Who? Oh, evil." And he sat down again. "Evil is the destructive urge. Not to be confused with mere wrong. Wrong is what the government doesn't like. Sometimes a thing can be wrong and evil at the same time—murder, for instance. But then it can be right to murder. Like you people going round killing the Vietnamese and so on. Evil called right."

"It wasn't right. Nobody said it was right."

"The government did. Get this straight. Right and wrong are fluid and interchangeable. What's right one day can be wrong the next. And vice versa. It's right to like the Chinese now. Before you started playing Ping-pong with them it was wrong. A lot of evil nonsense. What you kids need is some good food (there you are, see: good in non-ethical sense) and an idea of what good and evil are about."

"Well, go on, tell us."

"Nobody," said Enderby, having taken a swig, "has any clear idea about good. Oh, giving money to the poor perhaps. Helping old ladies across the street. That sort of thing. Evil's different. Everybody knows evil. Brought up to it, you see. Original sin."

"I don't believe in original sin." She was taking the bottle quite manfully now. "We're free."

Enderby looked on her bitterly, also sweating. It was really too hot to wear anything indoors. Damned unchangeable central heating, controlled by some cold sadist somewhere in the basement. Bitterly because she'd hit on the damned problem that he had to present in the poem. She ought to go away now and let him get on with it. Still, his duty. One of his students. He was being paid. Those brown bastards in whose hands he had left La Belle Mer would be shovelling it all from till to pocket. Bad year we had, señor. Had to near shut up bloody shop. He said carefully:

"Well, yes. Freeish. *Wir sind ein wenig frei.* Wagner wrote that. Gave it to Hans Sachs in *Die Meistersinger.*" And then: "No, to hell with it. Wholly free. Totally free to choose between good and evil. The other things don't matter—I mean free to drink a quart of whisky without vomiting and so on. Free to touch one's forehead with one's foot. And so forth."

"I can do that," she said. The latter. Doing it. That was the whisky, God help the ill-nourished child.

"But," Enderby said, ignoring the acrobatics. She didn't seem to be bothering to use her cassette thing any more. Never mind. "But we're disposed to do evil rather than good. History is the record of that. Given the choice, we're inclined to do the bad thing. That's all it means. We have to make a strong effort to do the good thing."

"Examples of evil," she said.

"Oh," said Enderby. "Killing for the sake of doing it. Torturing for pleasure—it always is that, though, isn't it? Defacing a work of art. Farting during a performance of a late Beethoven quartet. That must be evil because it's not wrong. I mean, there's no law against it."

"We believe," she said, sitting up seriously, checking the cassette machine and holding it out, "that a time will come when evil will be no more. She'll come again, and that will be the end of evil."

"Who's *she?*"

"Jesus, of course."

Enderby breathed deeply several times. "Look," he said. "If you get rid of evil you get rid of choice. You've got to have things to choose between, and that means good *and* evil. If you don't choose, you're not human any more. You're something else. Or you're dead."

"You're sweating just terribly," she said. "There's no need to wear all that. Don't you have swimming trunks?"

"I don't swim," Enderby said.

"It *is* hot," she said. And she began to remove her Coke-and-hamburger-stained sweater. Enderby gulped and gulped. He said:

"This is, you must admit, somewhat irregular. I mean, the professor and student relationship and all that sort of thing."

"You exhibited yourself. That's somewhat irregular too." By now she had taken off the sweater. She was, he supposed, decently dressed by beach standards, but there was a curious erotic difference between the two kinds of top worn. This was austere enough—no frills or representations of black hands feeling for the nipples. Still, it was *undress*. Beach dress was not that. He said:

"An interesting question when you come to think of it. If somebody's lying naked on the beach it's not erotic. Naked on the bed is different. Even more different on the floor."

"The first one's functional," she said. "Like for a surgical operation. Nakedness is only erotic when it's obviously not for anything else."

"You're quite a clever girl," Enderby said. "What kind of marks have I been giving you?"

"Two C's. But I couldn't do the sestina. Very old-fashioned. And the other one was free verse. But you said it was really hexameters."

"People often go into hexameters when they try to write free verse," Enderby said. "Walt Whitman, for instance."

"I have to get A's. I just have to." And then: "It *is* hot."

"Would you like some ice in that? I can get you some ice."

"Have you a cold Coke?"

"There you go again, with your bloody Cokes and 7-Ups and so on. It's uncivilised," Enderby raged. "I'll get you some ice." He went into the kitchen and looked at it gloomily. It *was* a bit dirty, really, the sink piled high. He didn't know how to use the washing-up machine. He crunched out ice cubes by pulling a lever. Ice cubes went tumbling into dirty water and old fat. He cleaned them on a dishrag. Then he put them into the GEORGIA tea mug and took them in. He gulped. He said: "That's going too far, you know." Topless waitresses, topless students. And then: "I forgot to wash a glass for you. Scatch on the racks," he added, desperately facetious. He went back to the kitchen and at once the kitchen telephone rang.

"Enderby?" It was an English voice, male.

"Professor Enderby, yes."

"Well, you're really in the shit now, aren't you, old boy?"

"Look, did you put her up to this? Who are you, anyway?"

"Ah, something going on there too, eh? This is Jim Bister from Washington. I saw you in Tangier, remember? Surrounded by all those bitsy booful brown boys."

"Are you tight?"

"Not more than usual, old boy. Look, seriously. I was asked by my editor to get you to say something about this nun business."

"What nun business? What editor? Who are you, anyway?" He was perhaps going too far in asking that last question again, but he objected to this assumption that British expatriates in America ought to be matey with each other, saying *in the shit* and so forth at the drop of a hat.

"I've said who I am. I thought you'd remember. I suppose you were half-pissed that time in Tangier. My newspaper is the *Evening Banner*, London if you've forgotten, what with your brandy and pederasty, and my editor wants to know what you—"

"What did you say then about pederasty? I thought I caught something about pederasty. Because if I did, by Jesus I'll be down there in Washington and I'll—"

"I didn't. Couldn't pronounce it even if I knew it. It's about this nun business in Ashton-under-Lyne, if you know where that is."

"You've got that wrong. It's here."

"No, that's a different one, old man. This one in Ashton-under-Lyne—that's in the North of England, Lancashire, in case you don't know—is manslaughter. Nunslaughter. Maybe murder. Haven't you heard?"

"What the hell's it to do with me anyway? Look, I distinctly heard you say pederasty—"

"Oh, balls to pederasty. Be serious for once. These kids who did it said they'd seen your film, the *Deutschland* thing. So now everybody's having a go at that. And one of the kids—"

"It's not mine, do you hear, and in any case no work of art has ever yet been responsible for—"

"Ah, call it a work of art, do you? That's interesting. And you'd call the book they made it from a work of art too, would you? Because one of the kids said he'd read the book as well as seen the film and it might have been the book that put the idea into his head. Any comments?"

"It's not a book, it's a poem. And I don't believe that it would be possible for a poem to— In any case, I think he's lying."

"They've been reading it out in court. I've got some bits here. May have got a bit garbled over the telex, of course. Anyway, there's this: 'From life's dawn it is drawn down, Abel is Cain's brother and breasts they have sucked the same.' Apparently that started him dreaming at night. And there's something about 'the gnarls of the nails in thee, niche of the lance, his lovescape crucified.' Very showy type of writing, I must say. They're talking about the danger to susceptible young minds and banning it from the Ashton-under-Lyne bookshops."

"I shouldn't imagine there's one bloody copy there. This is bloody ridiculous, of course. They're talking of banning the collected poems of a great English poet? A Jesuit priest, as well? God bloody almighty, they must all be out of their fucking minds."

"There's this nun dead, anyhow. What are you going to do about it?"

"Me? I'm not going to do anything. Ask the buggers who made the film. They'll say what I say—that once you start admitting that a work of art can cause people to start committing crimes, then you're lost. Nothing's safe. Not even Shakespeare. Not even the Bible. Though the Bible's a lot of bloodthirsty balderdash that ought to be kept out of people's hands."

"Can I quote you, old man?"

"You can do what the hell you like. Pederasty, indeed. I've got a naked girl in here now. Does that sound like pederasty, you stupid insulting bastard?" And he rang off, snorting. He went back, snorting, to his whisky and *pouffe*. The girl was not there. "Where are you?" he cried. "You and your bloody Jesus-was-a-woman nonsense. Do you know what they've done now? Do you know what they're trying to do to one of the greatest mystical poets that English poetry has ever known? Where are you?"

She was in his bedroom, he found to no surprise, lying on the circular bed, though still with her worker's pants on. "Shall I take these off?" she said. Enderby, whisky bottle in hand, sat down heavily on a rattan chair not too far from the bed and looked at her, jaw dropped. He said:

"Why?"

"To lay me. That's what you want, isn't it? You don't get much of a chance, do you, you being old and ugly and a bit fat. Well, anyway, you can if you want."

"Is this," asked Enderby carefully, "how you work for this bloody blasphemous Jesus of yours?"

"I've got to have an A."

Enderby started noisily to cry. The girl, startled, got off the bed. She went out. Enderby continued crying, interrupting the spasm only to swig at the bottle. He heard her, presumably now sweatered again and clutching her cassette nonsense that was partially stuffed with his woolly voice, leaving the apartment swiftly on sneakered feet. Then she, as it were, threw in her face for him to look at now that her body had gone—a lost face with drowned hair of no particular colour, green eyes set wide apart like an animal's, a cheese-paring nose, a wide American mouth that was a false promise of generosity, the face of a girl who wanted an A. Enderby went on weeping and, while it went on, was presented intellectually with several bloody good reasons for weeping: his own decay, the daily nightmare of many parcels (too many cigarette lighters that wouldn't work, too many old bills, unanswered letters, empty gin bottles, single socks, physical organs, hairs in the nose and ears), everyone's desperate longing for a final refrigerated simplicity. He saw very clearly the creature that was weeping—a kind of Blake sylph, a desperately innocent observer buried under the burden of *extension*, in which dyspepsia and sore gums were hardly distinguishable from past sins and follies, the great bloody muckheap of multiplicity (make that the name of the conurbation in which I live) from which he wanted to escape but couldn't. I've got to have an A. The sheer horrible innocence of it. Who the hell didn't feel he'd got to have an A?

It was still only eleven-thirty. He went to the bathroom and, mixing shaving cream with tears not yet dried, he shaved. He shaved bloodily and, in the manner of ageing men, left patches of stubble here and there. Then he shambled over to the desk and conjured St. Augustine.

*He strode in out of Africa, wearing a*
*Tattered royal robe of orchard moonlight*
*Smelling of stolen apples but otherwise*
*Ready to scorch, a punishing sun, saying:*
*Where is this man of the northern sea, let me*
*Chide him, let me do more if*
*His heresy merits it, what is his heresy?*
*And a hand-rubbing priest, olive-skinned,*
*Garlic-breathed, looked up at the*
*Great African solar face to whine:*
*If it please you, the heresy is evidently a*
*Heresy but there is as yet no name for it.*
*And Augustine said: All things must have a name,*
*Otherwise, Proteus-like, they slither and slide*
*From the grasp. A thing does not*
*Exist until it has a name. Name it*
*After this sea-man, call it after*
*Pelagius. And lo the heresy existed.*

What could be written sometime, Enderby suddenly thought, was a saga of a man's teeth—the Odontiad. The idea came to him because of this image of the African bishop and saint and chider, whose thirty-two wholesome and gleaming teeth he clearly saw, flashing like two ivory blades (an upper teeth and a lower teeth) as he gnashed out condemnatory silver Latin. The Odontiad—a poetic record of dental decay in thirty-two books. The idea excited him so much that he felt an untimely and certainly unearned gust of hunger. He sharply down-sir-downed his growling stomach and went on with his work.

*Pelagius appeared, north-pale, cool as one of*
*Britain's summers, to say, in British Latin:*
*Christ redeemed us from the general sin, from*
*The Adamic inheritance, the sour apple*
*Stuck in the throat (and underneath his solar*
*Hide Augustine blushed). And thus, my lord,*
*Man was set free, no longer bounden*
*In sin's bond. He is free to choose*
*To sin or not to sin, he is in no wise*
*Predisposed, it is all a matter of*
*Human choice. And by his own effort, yea,*
*His own effort only, not some matter of God's*
*Grace arbitrarily and capriciously*
*Bestowed, he may reach heaven, he may indeed*
*Make his heaven. He is free to do so.*
*Do you deny his freedom? Do you deny*
*That God's incredible benison was to*
*Make man free, if he wished, to offend him?*
*That no greater love is conceivable*
*Than to leave the creature free to hate*
*The creator and come to love the hard way*
*But always (mark this mark this) by his own*
*Will by his own free will?*
*Cool Britain thus spoke, a land where indeed a*
*Man groans not for the grace of rain, where*
*He can sow and reap, a green land, where*
*The God of unpredictable Africa is*
*A strange God*

It was no use. He ached with hunger. He went rumbling to the kitchen and looked at his untidy store cupboards. Soon he sat down to a new-rinsed dish of yesterday's stew reheated (chuck steak, onions, carrots, spuds, well-spiced with Lea and Perrin's and a generous drop or so of chili sauce) while there sang on the stove in deep though tepid fat a whole bag of ready-cut crinkled potato pieces and, in another pan, slices of spongy canned meat called Mensch or Munch or something. The kettle was on for tea.

To his surprise, Enderby felt, while sitting calm, relaxed, and in mildly pleasant anticipation of good things to come, a sudden spasm that was not quite dyspepsia. An obscene pain struck in the breastbone, then climbed with some difficulty into the left clavicle and, from there, cascaded like a handful of heavy money down the left upper arm. He was appalled, outraged, what had he done to deserve— He caught an image of Henry James's face for some reason, similarly appalled though in a manner somehow patrician. Then nausea, sweating, and very cruel pain took over entirely. What the hell did one do now? The dish of half-eaten stew did not tell him, except not to finish it. What was that about the something-or-other distinguished thing? Ah yes, death. He was going to die. That was what it was.

He staggered moaning and cursing about the unfairness to the living room (dying room?). Death. It was very important to know what he was dying of. Was this what was called a heart attack? He sat on a comfortless chair and saw pain dripping onto the floor from his forehead. His shirt was soaked. It was so bloody hot. Breathing was very difficult. He tried to stop breathing, but his body, ill as it was, was not going to have that. Forced to take in a sharp lungful, he found the pain receding. Not death then. Not yet. A warning only. There was a statutory number of heart attacks before the ultimate, was there not? What he was being warned against he did not know. Smoking? Masturbation? Poetry?

He smelt smoke. Ah, was that also a symptom, a dysfunctioning of the olfactory system or something? But no, it was the damned food he had left sizzling. He tottered back into the kitchen and turned everything off. Didn't feel much like eating now.

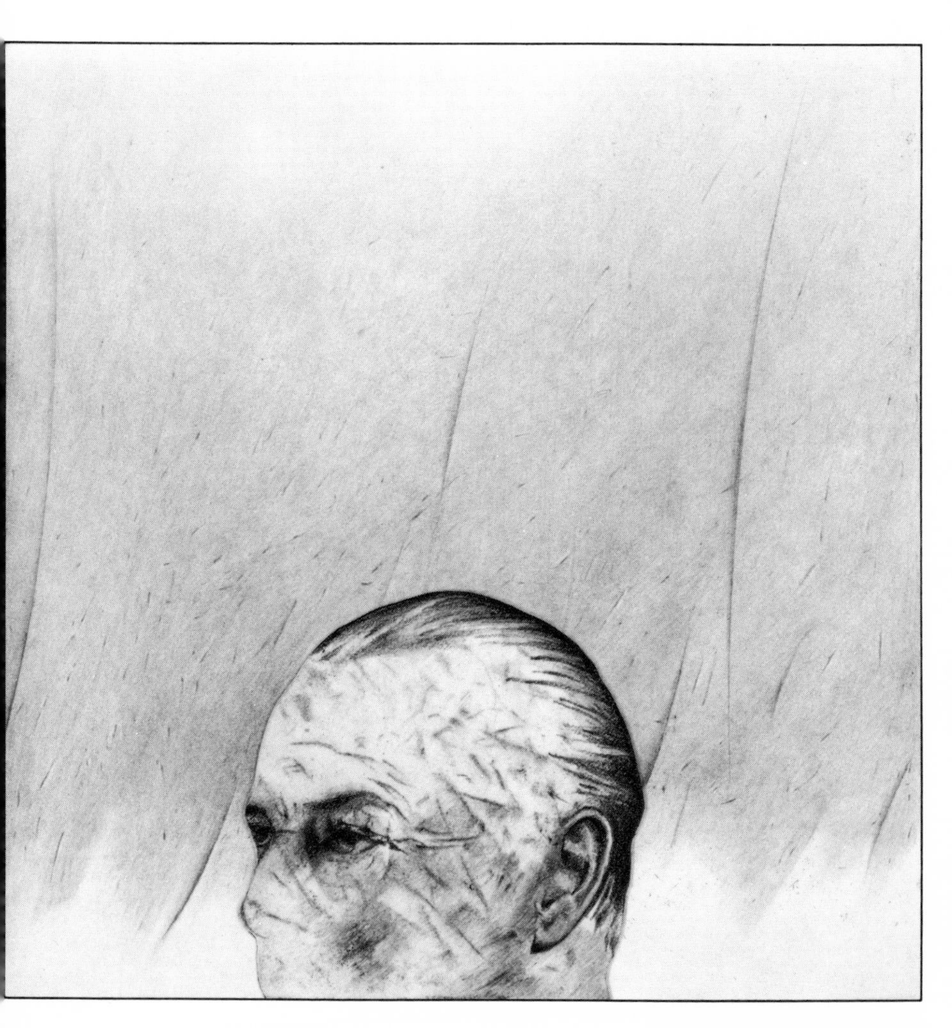

# FOUR

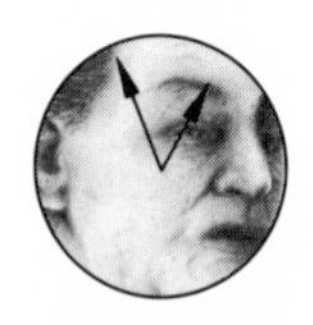

**ENDERBY** left the apartment and the apartment building itself with great caution, as though death, having promised sometime to present himself in one form, might (with a dirtiness more appropriate to life) now present himself in another. Enderby was well wrapped against what he took to be the February cold. He had looked from his twelfth-floor window to see fur caps as if this were Moscow, though also sun and wind-scoured sidewalks. Liverish weather, then. He was dressed in his old beret, woollen gloves, and a kind of sculpted Edwardian overcoat bequeathed by his old enemy Rawcliffe. Rawcliffe was long dead. He had died bloodily, fecally, messily, and now, to quote his own poem, practically his only own poem, his salts drained into alien soil. He had got death over with, then. He was, in a sense, lucky.

Perhaps posthumous life was better than the real thing. Oh God yes, I remember Enderby, what a man. Eater, drinker, wencher, and such exotic adventures. You could go on living without all the trouble of still being alive. Your character got blurred and mingled with those of other dead men, wittier, handsomer, themselves more vital now that they were dead. And there was one's work, good or bad but still a death-cheater. *Perennius aere*, and it was no vain boast even for the lousiest sonneteer that the Muse had ever farted onto. It wasn't death that was the trouble, of course, it was dying.

Enderby also carried, or was part carried by, a very special stick or cane. It was a swordstick, also formerly Rawcliffe's property. Enderby had gathered that it was illegal to go around with it in America, a concealed weapon, but that was the worst bloody hypocrisy he had ever met in this hypocritical country where everybody had a gun. He had not had cause to use the sword part of the stick, but it was a comfort to have in the foul streets that, like pustular bandages, wrapped the running sore of his university around. For corruption of the best was always the worst, lilies that fester, etc. What had been a centre of incorrupt learning was now a whorehouse of progressive intellectual abdication. The kids had to have what they wanted, this being a so-called democracy: courses in soul cookery, whatever that was, and petromusicology, that being teen-age garbage now treated as an art, and the history of black slavery, and innumerable branches of a subject called sociology. The past was spat upon and the future was ready to be spat upon too, since this would quickly enough turn itself into the past.

The elevator depressed Enderby to a vestibule with telescreens on the wall, each channel showing something different but always people unbent on violence or breaking in, it being too early in the day and probably too cold. A Puerto Rican named Sancho sat, in the uniform designed by Ms. Schwarz of the block police committee, nursing a submachine gun. He greeted Enderby in Puerto Rican and Enderby responded in Tangerine. The point was: where was the capital of Spanish these days? Certainly not Madrid. And of English? Certainly not London. Enderby, British poet. That was exact but somehow ludicrous. Wordsworth, British poet. That was ludicrous in a different way. When Wordsworth wrote of a British shepherd, as he did somewhere, he meant a remote shadowy Celt. Enderby went out into the cold and walked carefully, leaning on his swordstick, towards Broadway. This afternoon he had two classes and he wondered if he was up to either of them. The first was a formal lecture really in which, heretically, he taught, told, gave out information. It was minor Elizabethan dramatists, a subject none of the regular English

Department was willing—or, so far as he could tell, qualified —to teach. This afternoon he was dealing with—

At the corner of 91st Street and Broadway he paused, appalled. He had forgotten. But it was as if he had never known. There was a blank in that part of his brain which was concerned with minor, or for that matter, major Elizabethan drama. Was this a consequence of that brief heart attack? He had no notes, scorned to use them. Nobody cared, anyway. It was something to get an A with. He walked into Broadway and towards the 96th Street subway entrance, conjuring minor Elizabethans desperately—men who all looked alike and died young, black-bearded ruffians with ruffs and earrings. He would have to get a book on— But there was no time. Wait—it was coming back. Dekker, Greene, Peele, Nashe. The Christian names had gone, but never mind. The plays they had written? *The Shoemaker's Holiday, Old Fortunatus, The Honest Whore.* Which one of those syphilitic scoundrels had written those, and what the hell were they about? Enderby could feel his heart preparing to stop beating, and this could not, obviously, be allowed. The other class he had was all right—Creative Writing—and he had some of the ghastly poems they had written in his inside jacket pocket. But this first one— Relax, relax. It was a question of not trying too hard, not getting uptight, keeping your cool, as they said—very vague terms.

Reaching the subway entrance, moving as ever cautiously among muttering or insolent or palpably drugged people whom it was best to think of as being there mainly to demonstrate the range of the pigmentation spectrum, he observed, with gloom, shock, pride, shame, horror, amusement, and kindred emotions, that *The Wreck of the Deutschland* was now showing at the Symphony movie house. The 96th Street subway entrance he had arrived at was actually at the corner of 93rd Street. To see the advertising material of the film better, he walked, with his stick's aid, towards the matrical or perhaps seniorsororal entrance, and was able to take in a known gaudy poster showing a near-naked nun facing, with carmined lips opened in orgasm, the rash-smart sloggering brine. Meanwhile, in one inset tableau, thugs wearing swastikas prepared to violate five of the coifed sisterhood, Gertrude, lily, conspicuous by her tallness among them, and, in another, Father Tom Hopkins, S.J., desperately prayed, apparently having just got out of the bath to do so. Enderby felt his heart prepare, in the manner rather of a stomach, to react to all this, so he escaped into the dirty hell of the subway. A tall Negro with a poncho and a cowboy hat was just coming up, and he said no good to Enderby.

Hell, Enderby was thinking as he sat in one of the IRT coaches going uptownwards. Because we were too intellectual and clever and humanistic to believe in a hell didn't mean that a hell couldn't exist. If there were a God, he could easily be a God who relieved himself of the almost intolerable love he felt for the major part of his creation (on such planets, say, as Turulura 15a and Baa'rdnok and Juriat) by torturing forever the inhabitants of 111/9 Tellus 1706defg. A touch of pepper sauce, his palate entitled to it. Or perhaps an experiment to see how much handing out of torture he himself could tolerate. He had, after all, a kind of duty to his own infinitely variable supersensorium. Hamlet was right, naturally. Troubles the will and makes us rather. This little uptown ride, especially when the train stopped long and inexplicably between stations, was a fair miniature simulacrum of the ultimate misery —potential black and brown devils ready to rob, slice, and rape; the names of the devils blowpainted on bulkheads and seats, though never on advertisements (sacred scriptures of the infernal law)—JESUS 69, SATAN 127, REDBALL IS BACK.

Coming out of the subway, walking through the disfigured streets full of decayed and disaffected and dogmerds, he felt a sudden and inappropriate accession of well-being. It was as though that lunchtime spasm had cleared away black humours inaccessible to the Chinese black draught. Everything came back about minor Elizabethan drama, though in the form of a great cinema poster with a brooding Shakespeare in the middle. But the supporting cast was set neatly about—George Peele, carrying a copy of *The Old Wives' Tale* and singing in a fumetto about chopcherry chopcherry ripe within; poor cirrhotic Robert Greene conjuring Friars Bacon and Bungay; Tom Brightness-falls-from-the-air Nashe; others, including Dekker eating a pancake. That was all right, then. But wait—who were those other others? Anthony Munday, yes yes, a bad playbotcher but he certainly existed. Plowman? A play called *A Priest in a Whorehouse?* Deverish? *England's Might or The Triumphs of Gloriana?*

Treading through rack of crumpled protest handouts, desiccated leaves, beer cans, admitted with reluctance by a black armed policeman, he made his familiar way to the officially desecrated chapel which now held partitioned classrooms. Heart thumping, though fairly healthily, he entered his own (he was no more than five minutes late) to find his twenty or so waiting. There were Chinese, skullcapped Hebrews, a girl from the Coast who piquantly combined black and Japanese, a beer-fat Irishman with red thatch, an exquisite Latin nymph, a cunning know-all of the Kickapoo nation. He stood looking vaguely at them all. They lounged and ate snacks and drank from cans and smoked pot and looked back at him. He didn't know whether to sit or not at the table on which someone had chalked ASSFUCK. A little indisposed today, ladies and gentlemen. But no, he would doggedly stand. He stood. That bright Elizabethan poster swiftly evanesced. He gaped. All was blank except for imagination, which was a scurrying colony of termites. He said:

"Today, ladies and gentlemen, continuing our necessarily superficial survey of the minor Elizabethan dramatists—"

The door opened and a boy and a girl, wan and breathless from swift fumbling in the corridor, entered, buttoning. They sat, looking up at him, panting.

"We come to—" But who the hell did we come to? They waited, he waited. He went to the blackboard and wiped off some elementary English grammar. The chalk in his grip trembled, broke in two. He wrote to his astonishment the name GERVASE WHITELADY. He added, in greater surprise and fear, the dates 1559–1591. He turned shaking to see that many of the students were taking the data down on bits of paper. He was committed now: this bloody man, not yet brought into existence, had to have existed. "Gervase Whitelady," he said, matter-of-factly, almost with a smear of the boredom proper to mention of a name nauseatingly well known among scholars. "Not a great name—a name, indeed, that some of you have probably never even heard of—" But the Kickapoo know-all had heard of it all right: he nodded with superior vigour. "—But we cannot afford to neglect his achievement, such as it was. Whitelady was the second son of Giles Whitelady, a scrivener. The family had settled in Pease Pottage, not far from the seaside town we now call Brighton, and were supporters of the Moabite persuasion of crypto-reformed Christianity as far back as the time of Wyclif." He looked at them all, incurious lot of young bastards. "Any questions?" There were no questions. "Very well, then." The Kickapoo shot up a hand. "Yes?"

"Is Whitelady the one who collaborated with—what was the name of the guy now—Fenprick? You know, they did this comedy together—what the hell was the name of it—"

A very cunning young redskin sod, ought to be kept on

his reservation. Enderby was not going to have this. "Are you quite sure you mean Fenprick, er er—"

"Running Deer is the name, professor. It might have been Fencock. A lot of these British names sound crazy."

Enderby looked long on him. "The dates of Richard Fenpick," he said, "—note that it is *pick* not *prick*, by the way, er er—" Running Deer, indeed. He must sometime look through the admission cards they were supposed to hand in. "His dates are 1574–1619. He could hardly have collaborated with er—" He checked the name from the board. "Er Whitelady unless he had been a sort of infant prodigy, and I can assure you he was er not." He now felt a hunger to say more about this Fenpick, whose career and even physical lineaments were being presented most lucidly to a wing of his brain which, he was sure, had been newly erected between the heart attack and now. "What," he said with large energy and confidence, "we most certainly do know about er Fenpick is his instrumentality in bringing the Essex rebellion to a happy conclusion." To his shock the hand of the girl who had just come in with that oversexed lout there, still panting, shot up. She cried:

"Happy for whom?"

"For er everybody concerned," Enderby er affirmed. "It had happened before in history, English naturally, as Whatsisname's own er conveniently or inconveniently dramatised."

"Inconvenient for whom?"

"For er those concerned."

"What she means is," said the red-thatched beer-swollen Irish student, "that the movie was on last night. The Late Late Date-with-the-Great Show. What Bette Davis called it was *Richard Two*."

"*Elizabeth and Essex*," the buttoned girl said. "It failed and she had his head cut off but she cries because it's a Cruel Necessity."

"What Professor Enderby was trying to say," the Kickapoo said, "was that the record is all a lie. There was really a King Robert the First on the British throne, disguised as the Queen." Enderby looked bitterly at him, saying:

"Are you trying to take the— Are you *having a go?*"

"Pardon me?"

"The vital statistics," a young Talmudist said, pencil poised at the ready. "This Whitelady."

"Who? Ah, yes."

"The works."

"The works," Enderby said, with refocillated energy. "Ah, yes. One long poem on a classical theme, the love of er Hostus for Primula. The title, I mean the hero and heroine, are eponymous." He clearly saw a first edition of the damned poem with title page a horrid mixture of typefaces, fat ill-drawn nymphs on it, a round chop which said Bibliotheca Somethingorother. "Specimen lines," he continued boldly:

"*Then as the moon engilds the Thalian fields*
*The nymph her er knotted maidenhead thus yields,*
*In joy the howlets owl it to the night,*
*In joy fair Cynthia augments her light,*
*The bubbling conies in their warrens er move*
*And simulate the transports of their love.*"

"But that's beautiful," said the beautiful Latin nymph, unfat, un-ill-drawn, unknotted.

"Crap," the Talmudist offered. "The transports of *whose* love?"

"Theirs, of course," Enderby said. "Primavera and the er her lover."

"There were six plays," the Kickapoo said, "if I remember correctly."

"Seven," Enderby said, "if you count the one long attributed to er Sidebottom—"

"Crazy British names."

"But now pretty firmly established as mainly the work of er the man we're dealing with, with an act and a half by an unknown hand."

"How can they tell?"

"Computer work," Enderby said vaguely. "Cybernetic wonders in Texas or some such place." He saw now fairly clearly that he would have to be for the chop. Or no, no, I quit. This was intolerable.

"What plays?" the Chinese next to the Talmudist said, a small round cheerful boy, perhaps an assistant cook in his spare time or main time if this were his spare time.

"Yes," with fine briskness. "Take these down. *What do you lack, fair mistress?* A comedy, done by the Earl of Leicester's Men, 1588. *The Tragedy of Canicula,* Earl of Sussex's Men, the same year. A year later came *The History of Lambert Simnel,* performed at court for the Shrovetide Revels. And then there was, let me see—"

"Where can we get hold of them?" the melanonipponese said crossly. "I mean, there's not much point in just having the titles."

"Impossible," prompt Enderby said. "Long out of print. It's only important for your purpose that you know that Longbottom that is to say Whitelady actually existed—"

"But how do we know he did?" There were two very obdurate strains in this mixed Coast girl.

"Records," Enderby said. "Look it all up in the appropriate books. Use your library, that's what it's for. One cannot exaggerate the importance of er his contribution to the medium, as an influence that is, the influence of his rhythm is quite apparent in the earlier plays of er—"

"Mangold Smotherwild," the Kickapoo said, no longer sneeringly outside the creative process but almost sweatily in the middle of it. Enderby saw that he could always say that he had been trying out a new subject called Creative Literary History. They might even write articles about it: *The Use of the Fictive Alternative World in the Teaching of Literature.* Somebody called out: "Specimen."

"No trouble at all," Enderby said. "In the first scene of *Give you good den good my masters* you have a soliloquy by a minor character named Retchpork. It goes, as I remember, something like this:

"*So the world ticks, aye, like to a tocking clock*
*On th' wall of naked else infinitude,*
*And I am hither come to lend an ear*
*To manners, modes and bawdries of this town*
*In hope to school myself in knavery.*
*Aye, 'tis a knavish world wherein the whore*
*And bawd and pickpurse, he of the quatertrey,*
*The coneycatcher, prigger, jack o' trumps*
*Do profit mightily while the studious lamp*
*Affords but little glimmer to the starved*
*And studious partisan of learning's lore.*
*Therefore, I say, am I come hither, aye,*
*To be enrolled in knavish roguery.*
*But soft, who's this? Aye, marry, by my troth,*
*A subject apt for working on. Good den,*
*My master, prithee what o'clock hast thou,*
You I *would say, and* have *not* hast, *forgive*
*Such rustical familiarity*
*From one unlearn'd in all the lore polite*
*Of streets, piazzas and the panoply*
*Of populous cities—*

Something like that, anyway," Enderby said. "I could go on if you wished. But it's all a bit dull."

"If it's all a bit dull," the Irish one said, "why do we have to have it?"

"I thought you said he was influential," somebody else complained.

"Well, he was. Dully influential," the Kickapoo said.

"Dead at thirty-two," Enderby said, having checked with the blackboard data. "Dead in a duel or perhaps of the French pox or of a surfeit of pickled herrings and onions in vinegar with crushed peppercorns and sour ale or, of course, of the plague. It was a pretty bad year for the plague, I think, 1591." He saw Whitelady peering beseechingly at him, a white face from the shades, begging for a good epitaph. "He was nothing," Enderby said brutally, the face flinching as though from blows, "so you can forget about him. One of the unknown poets who never properly mastered their craft, spurned by the Muse." The whole luggage of Elizabethan drama was now, unfantasticated by fictional additions, neatly stacked before him. He knew what was in it and what wasn't. This Whitelady wasn't there. And yet, as the mowing face and haunted eyes, watching his, showed, in a sense he was. "The important thing," Enderby pronounced, "is to get yourself born. You're entitled to that. But you're not entitled to life. Because if you were entitled to life, then the life would have to be quantified. How many years? Seventy? Sixty? Shakespeare was dead at fifty-two. Keats was dead at twenty-six. Thomas Chatterton at seventeen. How much do you think you're entitled to, you?" he asked the Kickapoo.

"As much as I can get."

"And that's a good answer," Enderby said, meaning it, meaning it more than they, in their present stage of growth, could possibly mean it. He suddenly felt a tearful love and compassion for these poor orphans, manipulated by brutal statesmen and the makers of tooth-eroding sweet poisonous drinks and (his face blotted temporarily out that of anguished Whitelady) the bearded southern colonel who made it a virtue to lick chicken fat off your fingers. Schmaltz and Chutzpah. The names swam in, as from the Book of Deuteronomy. Who were they? Lawyers? He said: "Life is sensation, which includes thought, and the sensation of having sensation, which ought to take care of all your stupid worries about identity. Christ, Whitelady has identity. But what he doesn't have and what he never had is the sensation of having sensations. Better and cleverer people than we are can be invented." He saw how wrong he was about *perennius aere*. "But what can't be invented is," he said, directly addressing the couple who had come in late, "what you two were doing outside in the corridor."

The boy grew very red but the girl smirked.

"The touch of the skin of a young girl's breast. A lush-capped plush-kept sloe—"

"You got that the wrong way around," the Kickapoo said.

"Yes, yes," Enderby said, tired. And then, in utter depression, he saw who Whitelady was. He winked at him with his right eye and Whitelady simultaneously winked back with his left.

# FIVE

**AFTER** the lesson on Whitelady (lose sensation, he kept thinking, and I become a fictional character) Enderby walked with care, aware of a sensation of lightness in his left breast as though his heart (not the real one, the one of non-clinical traditional lore) had been removed. So sensation could lie, so whither did that lead you? His feet led him through a halfhearted student demonstration against or for the dismissal of somebody, a brave girl stripping in protest, giving blue breasts to the February post-meridian chill, to the long low building which was the English Department. Outside the office he shared with Assistant Professor Zeitgeist or some such name, there were black girl students evidently waiting for Professor Zeitgeist and beguiling their wait with loud manic music on a transistor radio. Enderby mildly said:

"Do switch that thing off, please. I have some work to do."

"Well, you goan work someplace else, man."

"This is, after all, my office," Enderby smiled, feeling palpitations drumming up. "This is, after all, the English Department of a University." And then: "Shut that bloody thing off."

"You goan fuck yoself, man."

"You ain't nuttin but shiiit, man."

Abdication. What did one do now—slap the black bitches? Remember the long servitude of their people and bow humbly? One of them was doing a little rutting on-the-spot dance to the noise. Enderby slapped the black bitch on the puss. No, he did not. He durst not. It would be on the front pages tomorrow. There would be a row in the United Nations. He would be knifed by the men they slept with. He said, smiling, rage boiling up to inner excoriation: "Abdication of authority. Is that expression in your primer of Black English?"

"Pip pip old boy," said the non-jigging one with very fair mock-British intonation. "And all that sort of rot, man."

"You go fuck yo own ass, man. You ain't nuttin but shiiiiit."

Enderby had another weapon, not much used by him these days. He gathered all available wind and vented it from a square mouth.

Rarkberfvrishtkrahnbrrryburlgrong.

The effort nearly killed him. He staggered into his office, saw mail on his desk, took it, and staggered out. The black girls, very ineptly, tried to give, in glee, his noise back to him. But their sense of body rhythm prevailed, turning it to oral tom-tom music. The radio took four seconds off from discoursing garbage of one sort to advertise garbage of another—male voice in terminal orgasm yelling sweet sweet sweet O Pan piercing sweet. Enderby went into the little lounge, empty save for shouting notices and a bearded man who looked knowingly at him. He opened his letters, chiefly injunctions to join things (BIOFEEDBACK BRETHREN GERONTOPHILIACS ANONYMOUS ROCK FOR CHRIST OUR SATAN THE THANATOLOGY MONTHLY), coming at length to a newspaper clipping sent, apparently out of enmity, by his publisher in London. It was from the *Daily Window* and was one of the regular hard-hitting noholdsbarred nononsense manofthepeople responsibilityofagreatnationalorgan addresses to the reader written by a staffman named Belvedere Fellows, whose jowled fierce picture led, like a brave over-age platoon officer, the heavy type of his heading. Enderby read: SINK THE DEUTSCHLAND! Enderby read:

*My readers know I am a man that faces facts. My readers know that I will sit through any amount of filthy film rubbish in order to report back fairly and squarely to my readers about the dangers their children face in a medium that increasingly, in the name of the so-called Permissive Society, is giving itself over to nudity, sex, obscenity and pornography.*

*Well, I went to see The Wreck of the Deutschland and confess that I had to rush to the rails long before the end. I was scuppered. Here all decent standards have finally gone Kaput. Here is the old heave-ho with a vengeance.*

*But enough has been said already about the appalling scenes of Nazi rape and the blasphemous nudity. We know the culprits: their ears are deafened to the appeals of decency by the crackle of the banknotes they are now so busily counting. There are certain quiet scoundrels whose names do not reach the public eye with the same tawdry glamour. Behind the film image lies the idea, lies the writer, skulking behind cigarette smoke and whisky in his ivory tower.*

*I say now that they must take their share of the blame. I have not read the book which the film is based on, nor would I want to. I noted grimly however that there were no copies the other day in my local library. My readers will be horrified however to learn that he is a Roman Catholic priest. This is what the liberalism of that great and good man Pope John has been perverted into.*

*I call now, equivocally and pragmatically, for a closer eye to be kept on the filth that increasingly these days masquerades as literature and even as poetry. The vocation of poet has traditionally been permitted to excuse too much—the lechery of Dylan Thomas and the drunken bravoing of Brendan Behan as well as the aesthetic perversions of Oscar Wilde. Is the final excuse now to be sought in the so-called priestly vocation? Perhaps Father Enderby of the Society of Jesus would like to reply. I have no doubt he would find an attentive congregation.*

Enderby looked up. The bearded man was still looking knowingly at him. He said something. Enderby said: "I beg your pardon?"

"I said: how are things in Jolly Old?"

Enderby could think of absolutely no reply. The two looked at each other fixedly for a long time, and the bearded man's jaw dropped progressively as if he were silently demonstrating an escalier of front vowels. Then Enderby sighed, got up, and went out to seek his Creative Writing class. Like a homer he tapped his way with his swordstick through the dirty cold and student knots to a building named for the inventor of a variety of canned soups, Warhall or somebody. On the second floor, to which he clomb with slow care, he found them, all ten, in a hot room with a long disfigured conference table. The Tietjens girl was there, drowned and sweatered. She had apparently told them everything, for they looked strangely at him. He sat down at the top or bottom of the table and pulled their work out of his inside pocket. He saw that he had given Ms. Tietjens a D, so he ballpointed it into a rather arty A. The rest shall remain as they are. Then he tapped his lower denture with the pen, plastic to plastic: tck tck, tcktck tck, TCK. He looked at his students, a mostly very untidy lot. They looked at him, lounging, smoking, taking afternoon beverages. He said:

"The question of sartorial approach is relevant, I think. When John Keats had difficulty with a poem he would wash and put on a clean shirt. The stiff collar and bow tie and tails of the concertgoer induce a tense attitude appropriate to the hearing of complex music. The British colonial officer would dress for dinner, even in the jungle, to encourage self-discipline. There is no essential virtue in comfort. To be relaxed is good if it is part of a process of systole and diastole. Relaxation comes between phases of tenseness. Art is essentially tense. The trouble with your er art is that it is not tense."

They all looked at him, not tense. Many of their names he still refused to take seriously—Chuck Szymanowski, for instance. His sole black man was called Lloyd Utterage, a very reasonable name. This man was very ugly, which was a pity and which Enderby deeply regretted, but he had very beautiful clothes, mostly of hot-coloured blanketing materials, topped with a cannibal-style wire-wool hairshock. He was very tense too, and this too Enderby naturally approved. But he was full of hate, and this was a bore. "I will not," Enderby said, turning to him, "read out all your poem, which may be described as a sort of litany of anatomic vilification. Two stanzas will perhaps suffice." And he read them with detached primness:

"*It will be your balls next, whitey,*
*A loving snipping of the scrotum*
*With rather rusty nail scissors,*
*And they tumble out then to be*
*Crunched underfoot crunch crunch.*

*It will be your prick next, whitey,*
*A loving chopping segmentally*
*With an already bloodstained meat hatchet,*
*And it will lie with the dog turds*
*To be squashed squash squash.*

"One point," he said. "If the prick is to be chopped in segments it will not resemble a dog turd. The writing of er verse does not excuse you from considerations of er—"

"He says it will lie *with* the dog turds," Ms. Tietjens said. "He doesn't say it will look like one."

"Yes yes, Sylvia, but—"

"Lydia."

"Of course, thinking of Ford. Sorry. But, you see, the word *it* suggests that it's still a unity, not a number of chopped bits of er penis. Do you see my point?"

"Yeah," Lloyd Utterage said, "but it's not a point worth seeing. The point is the hate."

"The poetry is in the pity," said Enderby. "Wilfred Owen. He was wrong, of course. It was the other way round. As I was saying, a unity and rather resembling a dog turd. So the image is of this er prick indistinguishable from—"

"Like Lloyd said," said a very spotty Jewish boy named Arnold Something, his hair also cannibalistically arranged, "it's the hate that it's about. Poetry is made out of emotions," he pronounced.

"Oh no," Enderby said. "Oh very much no. Oh very very very much no and no again. Poetry is made out of words."

"It's the hate," Lloyd Utterage said. "It's the expression of the black experience."

"Now," Enderby said, "we will try a little experiment. I take it that this term *whitey* is racialist and full of opprobrium and so on. Suppose now we substitute for it the word er *nigger*—" There was a general gasp of disbelief. "I mean, if, as you said, the point is the hate, then the hate can best be expressed—and, indeed, in poetry *must* be expressed—as an emotion available to the generality of mankind. So instead of either *whitey* or *nigger* you could have, er, *bohunk* or, say, *kike*. But *kike* probably wouldn't do—"

"You're telling me it wouldn't do," Chuck Szymanowski said.

"—Since the end words are disyllabic or er yes trisyllabic

but never monosyllabic. A matter of structure," Enderby said. "So listen. *It will be your balls next, nigger,* etc. etc. *It will be your prick next, nigger,* and so on. Now it is the structure that interests me. It's not, of course, a very subtle or interesting structure, as er Lloyd here would be the first to admit, but it is the structure that has the vitality, not all this nonsense about hate and so on. I mean, imagine a period when this kind of race-hate stupidity is all over, and yet the poem—*perennius aere,* you know—still by some accident survives. Well, it would be taken as a somewhat primitive but still quite engaging essay in vilification in terms of an anatomical catalogue, the structure objectifying and, as it were, cooling the hate. Comic too on the personal level—*It will be your balls next,* er *Crassus* or say *Lycidas.* Rather Catullan. You see." He smiled at them. Now they were really learning something.

"You think," Lloyd Utterage panted, "you're going to get away with that, man?"

"Away with what?" Enderby asked in honest and rather hurt surprise.

"Look," Ms. Tietjens said kindly, "he's British. He doesn't understand the ethnic agony."

"That's rather a good phrase," Enderby said. "It doesn't mean anything, of course. Like saying *potato agony.* Oh I don't know, though. The meanings of imaginative language are not the same as those of the defilers of language. Your President, for instance. The black leaders. Lesbian power, if such a thing exists—"

"He understands it," said Lloyd Utterage. "His people started it. Nigger-whippers despite their haw-haw-haw old top."

"Now that's interesting," Enderby said. "You see how the whipping image immediately begat in your imagination the image of a top? You have the makings of a word man. You'll be a poet someday when you've got over all this nonsense." Then he began to repeat *nigger-whipper* swiftly and quietly like a tongue-twister. "Prosodic analysis," he said. "Do any of you know anything about that? A British linguistic movement, I believe, so it may not have er gotten to you. *Nigger* and *whipper,* you see, have two vowels in common. Now note the opposition of the consonants—a rich nasal against a voiceless semivowel, a voiced stop against a voiceless. Suppose you tried *nigger-killer*. Not so effective. Why not? The *g* doesn't oppose well to the *l.* They're both voiced, you see, and so—"

"Maaaaaan," drawled Lloyd Utterage, leaning back in simulated ease, smiling crocodilewise. "You play your little games with yourself. All this shit about words. Closing your eyes to what's going on in the big big world."

Enderby got angry. "Don't call me *maaaaaan,*" he said. "I've got a bloody name and I've got a bloody handle to it. And don't hand me any of that *shit,* to use your own term, about the importance of cutting the white man's balls off. All that's going to save your immortal soul, *maaaaaan,* if you have one, is words. Words words words, you bastard," he crescendoed, perhaps going too far.

"I don't think you should have said that," said a mousy girl called Ms. Crooker or Kruger. "Bastard, I mean."

"Does he have the monopoly of abuse?" Enderby asked in heat. "It's he who's doing the playing about, anyway, with his bloody castration fantasies. He wouldn't have the guts to cut the balls off a pig. Or he might have. If it were a very little pig and ten big fellow melanoids held it down for him. I say," he then said, "that's good. *Fellow melanoids.*"

"I'm getting out of here," Lloyd Utterage said, rising.

"Oh no you're not," Enderby cried. "You're going to stay and suffer just like I am. Bloody cowardice."

"There's no engagement," Lloyd Utterage said. "There's no common area of understanding." But he sat down again.

"Oh yes there is," Enderby said. "I understand that you want to cut a white man's genital apparatus off. Well, come and try. But you'll get this sword in your black guts first." And he drew an inch or so of steel.

"You shouldn't have said black guts," Ms. Flugel or Crookback said. It was as though she were Enderby's guide to polite New York usage.

"Well," Enderby said, "they *are* black. Is he going to deny that now?"

"I never denied anything, man."

Suddenly the cannibal-haired kike or Jew, Arnold Something, began to laugh in a very high pitch. This started some of the others off: a bespectacled big sloppy student with a sloppy Viking moustache, for instance, began to neigh. Lloyd Utterage sulked, as did Enderby. But then Enderby, trying, which was after all his job here, to be helpful, said, "Greek *hystera*, meaning the womb. This shows, and this might possibly bring er here, our friend I mean, and myself into a common area of understanding, that etymology can get in the way of scientific progress, since Sigmund Freud's opponents in Vienna used etymology to confute his contention that hysteria, as now and here to be witnessed, could be found in the male as well as the female." Little of this could be heard over the noise. At length it subsided, and the sloppy Viking whose name was, Enderby thought and would now check from the papers before him and yes indeed it was, Sig Hamsun, said:

"And now how's about looking at *my* crap."

That very nearly made the cannibal Jew Arnold begin again, but he was rebuked ironically by Lloyd Utterage, who said: "This is serious, man, yeah serious, didn't you know it was serious, yeah serious, as you very well know."

Hamsun's crap, Enderby now saw again, looking through

it, was in no way sternly Nordic. To match its excretor it was rather sloppy and fungoid. Enderby recited it grimly however:

"*And as the Manhattan dawn came up*
*Over the skyline we still lay*
*In each other's arms. Then you*
*Came awake and the Manhattan dawn*
*Was binocularly presented in your*
*Blue eyes and in your pink nipples*
*Monostomatic heaven . . .*"

"What does that word mean?" a Ms. Hermsprong asked. "Mono something."

"It means," Enderby said, "that he had only one mouth."

"Well, we all know he only has one mouth. Like everybody else."

"Yes," Enderby said, "but she had two nipples, you see. The point is, I think, that he would have liked to have two mouths, you see. One for each nipple."

"No," Hamsun said. "One mouth was enough." He leered.

"Permit me," Enderby said coldly, "to tell you what your poem means. Such as it is."

"I wrote it, right?"

"You could just about say that, I suppose. It means fundamentally—which means this is the irreducible minimum of meaning—play between unitary and binary, that is to say: 1 dawn, 2 eyes, 2 nipples, 1 mouth. There's also colour play, of course—pink dawn in blue sky, two pink dawns in two blue eyes, two pink nipples, one pink mouth (also two pink lips), one blue heaven in pink nipples and pink mouth. You see? Well then, now we come to the autobiographical element or, if you like, the personal content. It's a childhood reminiscence.

The woman in it is your mother. You're greedy for her breasts, you want two mouths. Why should there be two of everything else—even the manifestly single city and single dawn—and only one sucking mouth? There." He sat back in post-exegetical triumph that the twin simmering murder in Lloyd Utterage's eyes did something to qualify. Ms. Tietjens said, in counter-triumph:

"If you want to know the truth, it was me."

"You mean you wrote it? You mean he stole it? You mean—"

"I mean I'm the woman in the poem, complete with two nipples. As you can vouch for."

"Look," Enderby said.

"He wrote it about me."

"What I mean is that I didn't bloody well ask to see them. Here, by the way, is *your* poem back. With an A on it. And a lousy poem it is, if I may say so. Coming into my apartment," he told the class, "and stripping off. Something to do with Jesus Christ being a woman. And you," he accused, "pretending to be lesbian."

"I never said I was that. You make too many false assumptions."

"Look," Enderby said in great weariness and with crackling energy. "All of you. A poem isn't important because of the biographical truth of the content."

"Look," countersaid the sloppy Nordic, "it was one way of keeping her there, can't you see that? She's there in that fucking poem forever. Complete with pink nipples."

"I'm not a thing to be kept," Ms. Tietjens said hotly. "Can't you see that attitude makes some of us go the way we do?"

"The point is," Enderby said, "that there are certain terrible urgencies." Lloyd Utterage guffaw-sneered in a way that

Enderby could only think of as *niggerish*. It was in the act of the formulation of the term that he realised with great exactitude the impossibility of his position. There was no communication; he was too old-fashioned; he had always been too old-fashioned. "The urgencies are not political or racial or social. They're, so to speak, semantic. Only the poetical enquiry can discover what language really is. And all you're doing is letting yourselves be ensnared into the irrelevancies of the slogan on the one hand and sanctified sensation on the other." So. Identity? Unimportant. Sensation? Unimportant. What the hell was left? "The urgent task is the task of conservation. To hold the complex totality of linguistic meaning within a shape you can isolate from the dirty world."

"The complex *what?*" Ms. Hermsprong asked. The rest of them looked at him as if he were, which he probably was, mad.

"Never mind," Enderby said. "You can't fight. You'll never prevail against the big bastards of computerised organisations that are kindly letting you enjoy the illusion of freedom. The people who write poems, even bad ones, are not the people who are going to rule. Sooner or later you're all going to go to jail. You have to learn to be alone—no sex, not even any books. All you'll have is language, the great conserver, and poetry, the great isolate shaper. Stock your minds with language, for Christ's sake. Learn how to write what's memorable. No, not write—compose in your head. The time will come when you won't even be allowed a stub of pencil and the back of an envelope." He paused, looking down. He looked up at their pity and wonder and the black man's hatred. "Try," he said lamely, "heroic couplets."

The cannibal Arnold said: "How long will you be staying?"

Enderby grinned citrously. "Not much longer, I suppose. I'm not doing any good, am I?" Nobody said anything. Hamsun did a slow and not ungraceful shrug. Chuck Szymanowski said:

"You're defeatist. You're anti-life. You're not helping any. The time will come later for all this artsy-shmartsy crap. But it's not now."

"If it's not now," Enderby said, "it's not ever." He didn't trouble to get angry at the designation of high and neutral art as crap. "You can't split life into diachronic segments." He would write a letter of resignation when he got back to the apartment. No, he wouldn't even do that. Today was what? Friday the twenty-sixth. There would be a salary cheque for him on Monday. Grab that and go. He was, by God, after all, despite everything, free. Ms. Cooper or Krugman said, kindly it seemed:

"What's your idea of a good pome?"

"Well," Enderby said. "Perhaps this:

"*Queen and huntress, chaste and fair,*
*Now the sun is gone to sleep,*
*Seated in thy silver chair,*
*State in wonted manner keep.*
*Hesperus entreats thy light,*
*Goddess excellently bright . . .*"

"Jesus," Lloyd Utterage said with awe. "Playing your little games, man." And then, blood mixed somewhere down there in his larynx: "You bastard. You misleading reactionary *evil* bastard."

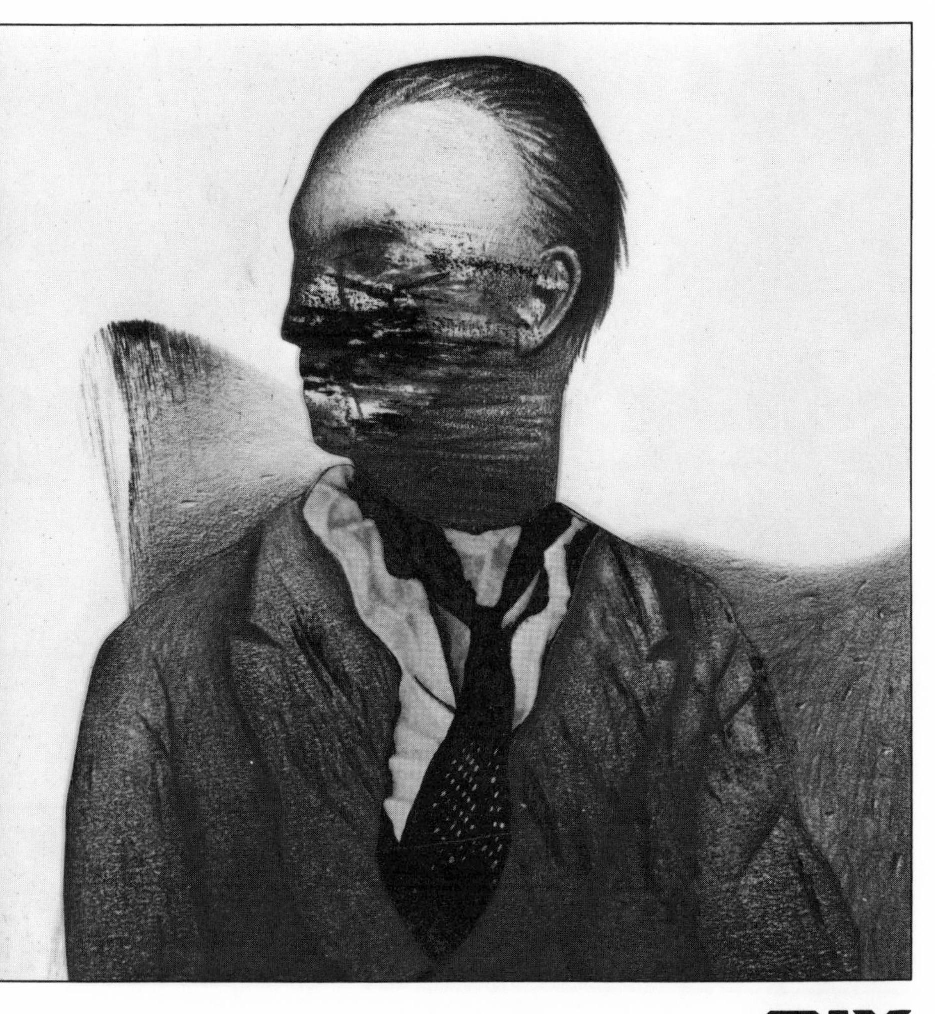

# SIX

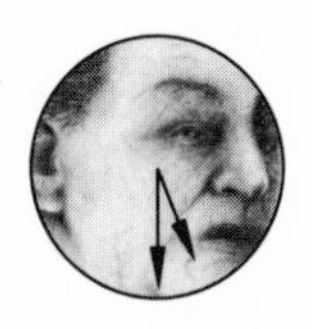

**ENDERBY** saw, in gloomy clarity, going back to 96th Street on the IRT, that the area of freedom was very small. *Ein wenig frei* was about right. He was not free, for instance, not to be messily beaten up by the black gang Lloyd Utterage had, in sincere and breathy confidence with much African vowel-lengthening, promised to unleash on him during the weekend. He was not free not to feel excruciating stabs in his calves, something probably to do with the silting up of the arteries, which had now come upon him as he embraced the metal monkey pole in the IRT train, all the seats having been taken by young black and brown thugs just out of school, who should by rights be forced to stand up for their elders. But he was free to leave America. A matter of booking on a plane to Madrid and then another to Tangier. Being free in this area, however, he decided not to make use of his freedom. Which meant he would not be free not to be messily beaten up etc. etc. Which meant he was *choosing* to be messily etc. They would bruise and rend his body, but there would be a thin clear as it were refrigerated self deep within, unbruisable and unrendable and, as it were, free. Augustine of Hippo, whom he now saw blanketed and shockhaired like Lloyd Utterage, was waiting for him back in the apartment to sort out other aspects of freedom for him. But, wait—he had to appear on a television talk show sometime this evening, didn't he? He must not forget that, he must keep track of the time. *Ein wenig frei* to speak out for Gerard Manley Hopkins, sufferer, mystic, artist, pre-Freudian.

As he let himself into the apartment, he was aware of the ghost of the cardiac attack, if that was what it was, earlier

—not shooting but already shot, a sort of bruised line of trajectory. It was obvious that he was intended to be doing some urgent thinking about death. He gloomed at the mess of the kitchen, lusting for a pint of strong tea and a wedge of some creature of Sara Lee's. He gave way to the lust defiantly, grumbling round the sitting room while the water boiled, searching for his ALABAMA mug. He found it eventually, full of warmish water that had once been ice. Soon he was able to sit on a *pouffe*, gorging sponge and orange cream out of one fist, the other holding the handle of the mug of mahogany tea like a weapon against Death, what time he looked at a children's cartoon programme on television. It was all talking animals in reds, blues, and yellows, but you could see the chained wit and liberalism of the creators escaping from odd holes in the fabric: that legalistic pig there was surely the Vice-President? Might it be possible to get the story of Augustine and Pelagius across in cartoon form?

Back in the study-bedroom with his draft, he saw how bad it was and how much work on it lay ahead. And yet he was supposed to start thinking of death. It was the leaving of things unfinished that was so intolerable. It was all very well for Jesus Christ, not himself a writer though no mean orator, to talk about thinking not of the morrow. If you'd started a long poem you had to think of the bloody morrow. You could better cope with the feckless Nazarene philosophy if you were like these scrounging dope-takers who littered the city. Sufficient unto the day is the evil thereof, as also the dope thereof.

*Augustine said: If the Almighty is also Allknowing,*
*He knows the precise number of hairs that will*
*fall to the floor*
*From your next barbering, which may also be your last.*
*He knows the number of drops of lentil soup*

*That will fall on your robe from your careless spooning*
*On August 5th, 425. He knows every sin*
*As yet uncommitted, can measure its purulence*
*On a precise scale of micropeccatins, a micropeccatin*
*Being, one might fancifully suppose,*
*The smallest unit of sinfulness. He knows*
*And knew when the very concept of man itched*
*within him*
*The precise date of your dispatch, the precise*
*Allotment of paradisal or infernal space*
*Awaiting you. Would you diminish the Allknowing*
*By making man free? This is heresy.*
*But that God is merciful as well as Allknowing*
*Has been long revealed: he is not himself bound*
*To fulfill foreknowledge. He scatters grace*
*Liberally and arbitrarily, so all men may hope,*
*Even you, man of the northern seas, may hope.*
*But Pelagius replied: Mercy is the word, mercy.*
*And a greater word is love. Out of his love*
*He makes man free to accept or reject him.*
*He could foreknow but refuses to foreknow*
*Any, even the most trivial, human act until*
*The act has been enacted, and then he knows.*
*So men are free, are touched by God's own freedom.*
*Christ with his blood washed out original sin,*
*So we are in no wise predisposed to sin*
*More than to do good: we are free, free,*
*Free to build our salvation. Halleluiah.*
*But the man of Hippo, with an African blast,*
*Blasted this man of the cool north . . .*

No no no, Enderby said to himself. It could not be done. This was not poetry. You could not make poetry out of raw doctrine. You had to find symbols, and he had no symbols.

The poem could not be written. He was free. The paper chains rustled off. He stuffed them into the wastebasket. Free. Free to start writing the *Odontiad*. Hence bound to start writing the *Odontiad*. Hence not free.

He sighed bitterly and went to the bathroom to start tarting himself up for the television show. Clean and bleeding, he put on garments bequeathed to him by Rawcliffe and stood, at length, to review himself at length in the long wall mirror near the bedroom door. Seedy Edwardian, recaller of dead glories, finale of Elgar's First Symphony belting out Massive Hope for the Future. There was an empire in those days, and it was assumed that the centre of the English language was London. Wealthy Americans were still humble provincials. Ichabod. He put on the sculpted overcoat and his beret and, swordstick pathetic in his feeble grip, went out.

The subway had not yet erupted into violent nocturnal life. His fellow-passengers on the downtown express to Times Square were as dimly ruminant as he, perhaps recalling dimly the glories of other departed empires—Ottoman, Austro-Hungarian, Pharaonic. But one black youth in a rutilant combat jacket saw drug-induced empires within—under the *pax alucinatoria* the rhomboid and spiral became one. Enderby looked again at the torn-off corner of the abandoned poem on which he had written *Live Lancing Show 46th Street or somewhere like that*. He had time, also two ten-dollar bills in his pocket. He would go to the Blue Bar of the Algonquin Hotel, a once very literary place, and have a quiet gin or so. He felt all right. The black tea and Sara Lee were worrying the heart combat troops: why was not the rutilant enemy scared?

He got out quite briskly at Times Square and walked down West 44th Street. In the lobby of the Algonquin there were, he saw, British periodicals on sale. He bought *The Times* and leafed through it standing. In a remote corner of it, he saw, a Member of Parliament was pleading for a special royal commission to clean up the Old Testament. Dangers even in great classics, provocation to idle and affluent youth etc. In the Blue Bar there were some conspiratorial and lecherous customers at tables, but seated on a bar stool was a rather loud man whose voice Enderby seemed to recognise. Good God, it was Father Hopkins himself. No, the man who played him in the film. What was his name now?

"So I said to him *up yours*, that's what I said."

"That's it, Mr. O'Donnell."

Coemgen (pronounced Kevin) O'Donnell, that was the man. Enderby had met him briefly at a little party after the London preview, when he had been affably drunk. No coincidence that he was here now: the Algonquin took in actors as much as writers. Sitting at a stool two empty stools away from O'Donnell, Enderby asked politely for a pink gin. O'Donnell, hunched to the counter, heard the voice, swivelled gracelessly, and said:

"You British?"

"Well, yes," Enderby said. "British-born but, like yourself I presume, living in exile. Look, we've already met."

"Never seen you before in my life." The voice was wholly American. "Lots of guys like you, seen me in the movies, assume acquaintanceshhh. Ip. You British?"

"Well, yes. British-born but, like yourself I presume, living in."

"You said all that crap already, buster. All I asked was a straight queschhh. Un. Okay, you're British. Needn't keep on about it. No need to eggs hhhibit the flag tattooed on your ass. And all that sort of. What? What?"

"The film," Enderby said. "The movie. *The Wreck of the Deutschland.*"

"I was in it. That was my movie." He thrust his empty tumbler rudely towards the bartender. He was most unpriestlike in his dress, glistening cranberry suit, violet silk, shoes that Enderby took to be Gucci. The face was a rugged corner-boy's, apt for some slum baseball-with-the-kids Maynooth-type priest, but hardly for the delicate intellectual unconscious pederast ah-my-dear Hopkins.

"The point is," Enderby said, "that I too was in it in a sense. It was my idea. My name was among the credits. Enderby," he added, to no applause. "Enderby," to not even recognition. Coemgen O'Donnell said:

"Yeah. I guess it had to be somebody's idea. Everything is kind of built on the idea of some unknown guy. You seen the figures in this week's *Variety?* Sex and violence, always the answer. But the guy that wrote the book was not like the guy I played in the movie. No, sir. The original Father Hopkins was a fag."

"A priest a fag?" the bartender said. "You don't say."

"There are priests fags," O'Donnell said. "Known several. Have it off with the altar boys. But in the movie he's normal. Has it off with a nun." He nodded gravely at Enderby and said: "You British?"

"Listen," Enderby said, "Gerard Manley Hopkins was not a homosexual. At least not consciously. Certainly not actively. Sublimation into the love of Christ perhaps. A theory, no more. A possibility. Of no religious or literary interest, of course. A love of male beauty. *The Bugler's First Communion* and *The Loss of the Eurydice* and *Harry Ploughman.* Admiration for it. 'Every inch a tar, of the best we boast our sailors are.' 'Hard as hurdle arms, with a broth of goldish flue.' What's wrong with that, for Christ's sake?"

"Broth of goldfish my ass," O'Donnell said. "Has that guy from the front office come yet?" he asked the bartender.

"He'll come in here, Mr. O'Donnell. He'll know where you are. If I was you, sir, I'd make that one the last. Until after the show, that is."

"Show?" Enderby said. "Are you by any chance on the —" He consulted the tear-off from his pocket. "Live Lancing Show?"

"Hey, that's good. Sperr would like that. Not that it's live, old boy, old boy. Nothing's live, not any more." And then: "You British?"

"I've said already that I—"

"You a fag? Okay okay. That's not what I was going to ask. What I was going to ask was— What was I going to ask?" he asked the bartender.

"Search me, Mr. O'Donnell."

"I know. Something about a bugle boy. What was that about a bugugle boy?"

"*The Bugler's First Communion?*"

"That's it, I guess. Now this proves that he was a fag. You British? Yeah yeah, asked that already. That means you know the town of Oxford, where the college is, right? It was my father."

"*What?*"

"Got that balled up, I guess. Big army barracks there. Cow cow cow something."

"Cowley?"

"Right, you'd know that, being British. Another scatch on the—"

"Sorry, Mr. O'Donnell. You yourself give me strict instructions when you started."

"Okay okay, gotta be with old Can Dix. Sending a limousine."

"Who? What?"

"Sending a car around. This talk show."

"I," Enderby said, "am on the other one, the Spurling one. What," he said with apprehension, "are you going to tell them?"

"Listen, old boy old boy, not finished, had I, right?

Right. It was my mother's father. British, with an Irish mother. Sent him off to be good Catholic. Right? One hell of a row, father was Protestant."

"Yes," Enderby said. " 'Born, he tells me, of Irish/ Mother to an English sire (he/ Shares their best gifts surely, fall how things will).' "

"Not finished, had I, right?"

"Sorry."

"No need to be sorry. Never regret anything, my what the hell do you call it slogan, right? Went over to Ireland with my mother's father's mother, he was my mother's father, you see that?"

"Right."

"Married Irish, the British all got smothered up. Well, that was his story."

"What was his story?"

"Had him down there in what do you call it presbyt presbyt, his red pants off of him and gave him, you know, the stick. Met him again in Dublin when he was some sort of professor, reminded him of it. Made him very sick. Very sick already."

"Oh God," Enderby said.

*O now well work that sealing sacred ointment!*
*O for now charms, arms, what bans off bad*
*And locks love ever in a lad!*
*Let mé though see no more of him,*
  *and not disappointment*
*Those sweet hopes quell whose least me*
  *quickenings lift . . .*

"I can't believe it," Enderby said. "I won't." He had intimations of a renewal of quasi-lethal pains ready to shoot from chest to clavicle to arm. No, he wouldn't have it. He frightened the promise away with a quick draught of gin. "So," he said. "You're going to tell them all about it?"

"Not that," O'Donnell said. "Crack a few gags about nuns. I was with this dame in a taxi and she was a nun. She'd have nun of this and nun of that."

"What a filthy unspeakable world," Enderby said. "What defilement, what horror."

"You can say that again. Ah, Josh. It *is* Josh? Sure it's Josh. How are things, Josh? How's the kids and the missus? The old trouble-and-strife, our British friend here would say." His Cockney was tolerable. "A cap of Sara Lee and dahn wiv yer rahnd the ahzes."

"Getting married next month," this Josh said unrelatedly. He looked Armenian to Enderby, hairy and with an ovine profile.

"Is that right, is that really right, well I sure am happy for you, Josh. Our friend here," O'Donnell said, "has been talking about our movie, *Kraut Soup*." He stood up and appeared not merely sober but actually as though he had just downed a gill of vinegar. He was, after all, an actor. Could you then believe anything he said or did? But how did he know about the barracks at Cowley? "What defilement, what horror," he said, in exactly Enderby's accent and intonation.

"Is that right?" Josh said. "We'd best be on our way, Mr. O'Donnell. There may be a fight with the autograph hounds."

"Say that story isn't true," Enderby begged. "It *can't* be true."

"My granddaddy swore it was true. He always remembered the name. We had a Mrs. Hopkins who cleaned for us. He had nothing against priests, he said. He was a real believer all his life."

*Though this child's drift / Seems by a divíne doom chánnelled, nor do I cry / Disaster there . . .*

"The car's waiting, Mr. O'Donnell."

"And he saw it wasn't real sexual excitement. Not like he'd seen in the barracks. It was all tied up with— Well, his hands were shaking with the joy of it, you know." Low-latched in leaf-light housel his too huge godhead. *Too huge*, my dear. "Come on, Josh, let's go. He was only a kid but he saw that." He nodded very soberly. "So I had to do the part, I guess." O'Donnell waved extravagantly to the bartender and Guccied out, shepherded by Josh. Enderby had another pink gin, feeling pretty numb. What did it matter, anyway? It was the poetry that counted. I am gall, I am heartburn, God's most deep decree/ Bitter would have me taste. And no bloody wonder.

The ways leading to the television place on 46th Street were warming up nicely with the threat of violence. Violence in itself is not bad, ladies and gentlemen. In a poem you would be entitled to exploit the fortuitous connotations—violins, viols, violets. We need violence sometimes. I feel very violent now. Beware of barbarism—violence for its own sake. It was a little old theatre encrusted with high-voltage light bulbs. There was a crowd lining up outside, waiting to be the studio audience. They would see themselves waving to themselves tomorrow night, the past waving to the future. The young toughs in control wore uniform blazers, rutilant with a monogram SL, and they would not at first let him in by the stage door: you line up with the rest, buster. But then his British accent convinced them that he must be one of the performers. Then they let him in.

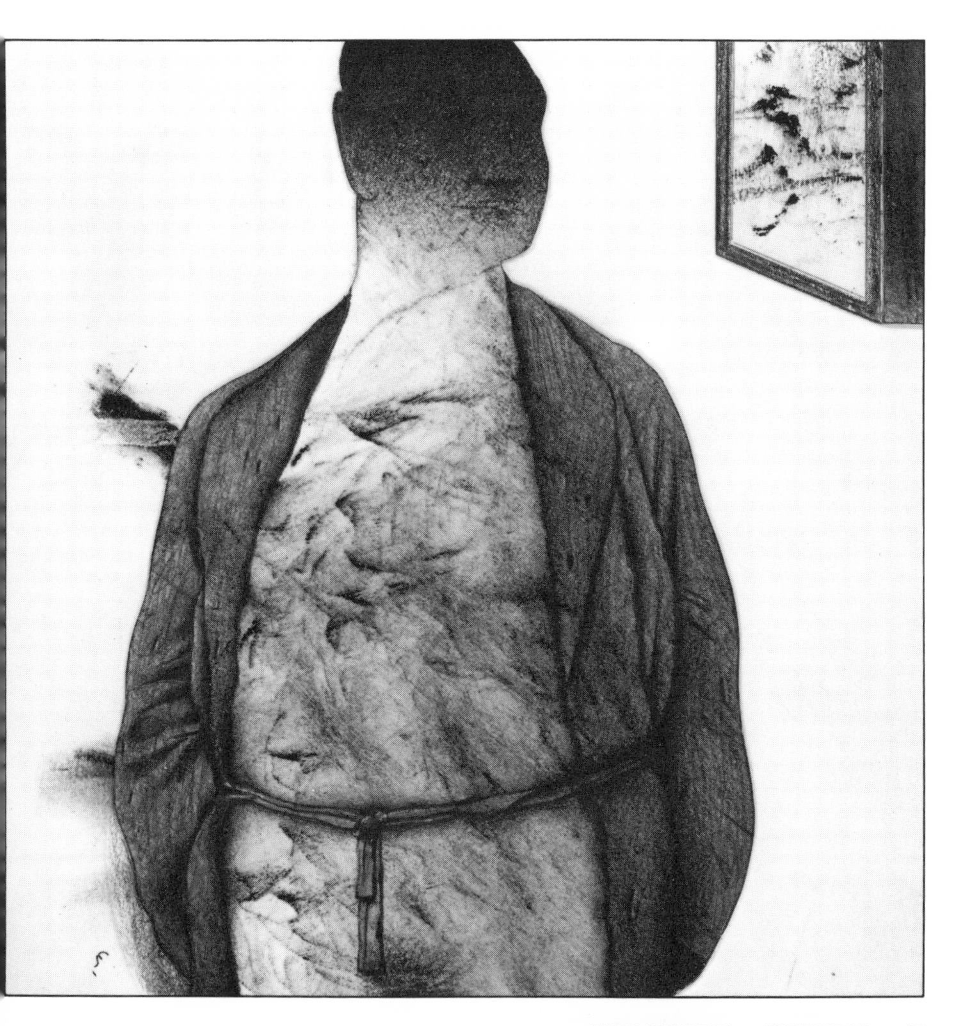

# SEVEN

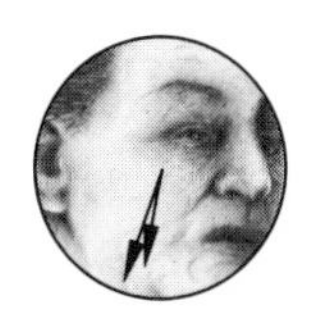

PARTIAL TRANSCRIPT OF SPERR LANSING SHOW B/3/57. RECORDED BUT NOT USED. RESERVE 2 (AUSTRALIAN TOUR) PUT OUT AS LAST MINUTE SUBSTITUTE.

SPERR: Thank you thank you (*No response to applause killer*) thank you thank you well this is what Id call a real dose of the (*Laughter and Applause*) I didnt say that I didnt say no I didnt. Seriously though (*Laughter*) the rise in prices. I went to a new barber yesterday and before I even sat down he said thatll be one dollar fifty (*Laughter*). Thats cheap I told him for a haircut (*Laughter*). That he said is for the estimate (*Laughter and Applause*). Seriously though (*Laughter*) the way they speak English in New York (*Laughter*). I saw two men at Kennedy Airport the other day and one said to the other When are you leaving. The other said I am leaving in the Bronx (*Laughter and Applause*). I have a new tailor did I tell you or should I say I HAD a new tailor (*L*). I took the suit back and said this doesnt fit. Sure it doesnt fit he said. Youre not wearing it right (L). You have to stick out your left hip and your right shoulder and bend that knee a bit (*L and A*). Then it fits nice (*L*). So I did as he said (*Visual. L and A*) and was walking along 46th Street when two doctors came by and I heard one say to the other Look at that poor feller a terrible case of deformity (*L*). Right says the other. The suit fits nice though (*L and prolonged A*). Seriously though clients and customers anybody here tonight from Minneapolis and St. Paul (*A and Jeers*). I thought not (*L*). That means I cant say I went out with a girl from up there (*L*). She was called the tail of two cities (*Prolonged L and A. SPERR shouts over*). Be right back. A great guest list tonight folks desirable Ermine Elderley Jake Summers Prof (*Premature start commercial break*)

SPERR: So if you want to stay slim and feel overfed girls try it. My first guest tonight is a famous British poet at present visiting professor at . . . University of Manhattan. Weve asked him to come and say something about a movie that was all his idea and is at present causing a riot in the movie houses of the civilized world. Ladies and gentlemen—Professor Fox Enderby (*Applause card Applause. Visual unrehearsed guest trips on wire. A and L*).

SPERR: Must say we all admire the suit Professor Enderby (A). A bit of Oldy England (A).

ENDERBY: (*Unintelligible*) right name.

SPERR: Oh I see just the initials. Pardon me. Well an O is a zero right. And a zeros nothing right. So its just an F and an X. With nothing between. Like I said. F O X (*Prolonged A*).

ENDERBY: (*Unintell*).

SPERR: Are you married, professor? (*Headshake no*) Do you have children? (*L*).

ENDERBY: A wise child knows his own (?)

SPERR: What I want to say is do you would you like children of yours to see a movie like Wreck of the Deutschland.

ENDERBY: Anybody can see what the hell they like for all I care. Anybodys children. Cluding (?) yours.

SPERR: I have a daughter of six (A). You wouldn't object to her seeing a movie of nuns being er (*Prolonged A*).

ENDERBY: Not the point. The point is to have a world in which nuns are not. Then it wouldnt be in films. Then thered be no danger of your daughter. Besides its adults only.

SPERR: Maybe. But there are disturbing reports of the young seeing the film and then committing atrocities (A).

ENDERBY: What the hell are they clapping for. Because of the atrocities. Would your six year old daughter go round raping nuns.

SPERR: No but shed be disturbed and maybe wake up crying with nightmares (A). We like to protect our children professor (*Very prol.* A).

ENDERBY: And wheres it got (?) you protecting them. More juvenile violence in America than anywhere else in the world. Not that I object to violence (*Audience protest*). You cant change things without violence. You baggers (?) were violence when you broke away from us in 1776. Not blaming you for that of course. You wanted to do it and were term into do it (??). You were wrong of course. Might still be a bit of law and order if you were still colonial territory. Not ready for self gov (*Audience protest and some* A).

SPERR: Your attitude ties up with your dress professor (*Prol.* A). I understand then that youre very patriotic. But youre not living in Britain are you.

ENDERBY: Cant stand the bloody place. Americanized. The past is the only place worth living in. Imaginary past. Lets get back to what we were talking about before you introduced irreverences (?).

SPERR: You did it not me (A).

ENDERBY: People always blame art literature drama for their own evil. Or other peoples. Art only imitates life. Evils already there. Original sin. Curious thing about America is that it was founded by people who believed original sin and also priesty nation (???) but then you had to watch for signs of gods grace and this was in commercial success making your own way building heaven on earth and so on and this led to American plagiarism (?).

SPERR: What words that professor.

ENDERBY: A British monkey called Morgan in Greek Plage us (??????) taught no national pensity (?) to evil. Errorsy (?). Evils in everybody. Desire to kill rape destroy mindless violence . . .

SPERR: I thought you said you liked violence (*Prol. A*).

ENDERBY: Never said that you silly bagger (?). Never said mindless MINDLESS violets. Constructive different.

SPERR: Oh I see sorry. Take a break now. Be right back. Dont go away (*Prol. A. Music pomp circus dance* (?)). (*Commercial break*)

SPERR: Oh there you are. Hi. My next guest is also a professor youve met often on the show. Expert on human behavior and author of many books such as er The Human Engine Waits will you please welcome back professor of psychology Stations of the Cross university Ribblesdale NY Man Balaglas (*Applause card Applause. Prof Balaglas*).

SPERR: Well hi. Its been quite some time professor.

ENDERBY: What did you say it was called.

BALAGLAS: What.

ENDERBY: This university where youre at. I didnt quite catch the.

BALAGLAS: Stations of the Cross.

ENDERBY: Catholic.

BALAGLAS: Theres Protestants there too. Jews. Fifth Day Adventists. What youd call ecommunionicle (?).

SPERR: And do you like violence too professor (*A and some L*).

ENDERBY: I never said I liked the bloody thing. Mindless I said.

BALAGLAS: Most emphatic no. The great scourge of our age and one of the most urgent of our needs is to laminate (?) it and that is what my own department along with others in other universities regards as research priority (*Pause then some* A).

ENDERBY: Youll never get rid of it. Original sin.

BALAGLAS: I would there most emphatic disagree an urgent problem we have to make our cities places where people can walk at night without getting mugged and raped and killed all the time (A).

ENDERBY: (*Unintell*) all the time.

SPERR: And how can this be done professor.

BALAGLAS: Positive rain forcemeat (?). Instructive urge is not killed (kwelled?) by prison or punishment. Brainwashing that is to say negative through fear of pain already tried but is fundamentally inhuman (e?). We must so condition human mind that reward is expected for doing good not the other way about.

ENDERBY: What other way about.

SPERR: Like he said professor. Psychology.

ENDERBY: A lot of simple (sinful?) bloody nonsense. You take the filament of human choice out of ethnical decisions. Men should be free to choose good. But theres no choice if theres only good. Stands to region there has to be evil as well.

BALAGLAS: I emphatic disagree. What does inhabited or unconditioned human choice go for. For too much rape and mugging (A).

ENDERBY: In other words original sin. Which leads us to the stations of the cross.

BALAGLAS: Pardon me.

ENDERBY: Youre not Christian then.

BALAGLAS: An irreverent question. Were all in this together (A).

SPERR: You think its possible then professor that people can be made to be good by er positive er.

BALAGLAS: Right. Its happening already. Volunteers in our prisons. Also in our universities. Stations of the Cross is proud of its volunteer record.

SPERR: Well thats just (*Interrup by loud* A).

ENDERBY: What you mean is that the community is more important than the individual.

BALAGLAS: Pardon me.

ENDERBY: Stop saying bloody pardon me all the time. What I said was that you think human beings should give up freedom to choose so that the community can be free of violence (A).

BALAGLAS: Right. Youve said it loud and clear professor. Bloody clear if I may borrow your own er locomotion (???). The individual has to sacrifice his freedom to some extent for the benefit of his fellow citizens (*Prolonged A*).

ENDERBY: Well I think its bloody monsters (?). Human beings are defined by freedom of choice. Once you have them doing what theyre told is good just because theyre going to get a lump of sugar instead of a kick up the ahss (?!) then ethnics no longer exists. The State could tell them it was good to go off and mug and rape and kill some other nation. Thats what its been doing. Look at your bloody war in . . .

SPERR: Well be right back after this important message. Dont go away folks. Be right b (*Prem start comm break*) (*Music. Band on Camera. Audience shots*)

SPERR: This is the Sperr Lansing Show. Be right back after this station break.

(*Station break*)

SPERR: Were talking with two professors Professor Balaglas psychologist and Professor er Endivy British poet. Professor Balaglas . . .

BALAGLAS: Call me Man (*Pause then A*). Representative Man (*P then A*).

ENDERBY: Whats that short for. I knew you werent a bloody Christian.

SPERR: Do you believe professor that movies and books and er art can influence young people to violence rape mugging and so on (*A*).

BALAGLAS: There is I would consider ample proof that the impressionable and not merely those in the younger age groups can be incited to antisocial behavior by the artistic representation of er antisocial acts. There was the instance in the township of Inversnaid NY not too far from Ribblesdale where as you know I am at present on the faculty of the university there of the young man who killed his uncle and said that seeing Sir Laurence Oliviers movie of Hamlet had influenced him to perform the crime.

ENDERBY: How old was he. I asked how old was.

BALAGLAS: About thirty. And very unbalanced.

ENDERBY: And had his uncle just married his mother (*L*). His mother. Not his uncles mother (*L*).

BALAGLAS: I dont recollect as much. It was just the killing of his uncle as in this movie. And also if I recollect rightly that also comes in the play on which the movie was based.

ENDERBY: Shakespeare.

SPERR: Thats right. And would you believe in the restricting of the viewing of professor.

ENDERBY: Of course not. Bloody ridiculous idea.

SPERR: I meant the other professor professor (*L and A*).

BALAGLAS: Well as we are committed to control of the violentment (?) and as works of art and movies and the like are part of it then for the sake of society there must be control. There are too many dirty books and movies and also violent ones (*A*).

ENDERBY: This is bloody teetotal Aryan (??) talk. You mean that kids wouldnt be allowed to see or read Hamlet because they might go and kill their uncles. Ive never in my life heard such bloody stupid actionary (?) talk. Why by Christ man

BALAGLAS: Thats right Man thats my name (*L and A*). Call me Man by all means but cut out the blasph (*Very loud A*).

ENDERBY: But bagger (?) it man you idiot I mean that would mean that nobody could read anything not even Alice in Windowland (?) because it says Off with his Head and the Wizard of Oz because of the wicked witch is

BALAGLAS: I do not know what standards of etiquette prevail in your part of the world Professor Elderley but I do most strenuously object to being called idiot (*Very loud A*).

SPERR: And at that opportune moment we take a break. Stay with us folks (*A*).

(*Commercial break*)

SPERR: Professor Balaglas made an interesting slip of the tongue folks which weve just been discussing during the break.

ENDERBY: I still say that he was trying to be bloody insulting. A man cant help his age.

SPERR: Right. Because if a girls name was ever improper that is to say not appropriate to what she is then the name of my next guest must be. Beautiful charming talented and above all YOUNG star of such movies as The Leaden Echo Mortal Beauty Rockfire and just about to be released Manshape here she is folks Ermine Elderley (*Very loud and sustained Applause also male whistles as she comes on kisses Sperr and Prof Balaglas not Prof Enderby sits down*).

SPERR: Wow (*L and A*).

ENDERBY: I see so youre Elderley. I thought he was trying to take the (*Unintell* piece? pass?)

ERMINE: Sure I am. How young do you like em (*L and A*).

ENDERBY: What I meant was (*Not heard under L and A*)

SPERR: Ermine if I may call you Ermine

ERMINE: Just buy it for me sweetie (*L and A*). I apologize. You always have done before baby (*L and A*). Called it me I mean (*L and A*).

SPERR: How would you like to be raped (*Very sust L with A lot of visual L L and again L*). I meant in a movie of course. Seriously (*L*).

ERMINE: Seriously yes. If I was playing that sort of part okay but I dont think I would oh I might if there was a kind of you know moral lesson and the guy gets his comeuppance after or before he really gets under way his teeth knocked out that sort of thing not shooting shootings too good. But I wouldnt have it if I was playing a nun like in this German movie. Thats irreligious.

ENDERBY: Look Im not trying to defend it. What she calls this German movie. As a matter of fact its not allowed to be shown in Germany.

SPERR: No Deutschland for Deutschland right (*L*).

ENDERBY: I have to make this clear dont I.

ERMINE: You should know brother (*L*).

ENDERBY: The film is very different from the poem.

SPERR: What poem is that.

ENDERBY: Why the poem its based on. By Gerald Mann Leigh.

ERMINE: You mean no rape in the poem (*L*). Well what do they do in the poem pluck daffodils (*L*).

**
** Enderby, sweating hard under the lights and the awareness of his unpopularity, looked at this hard woman who exhibited great sternly supported breasts to the very periphery of the areola and was dressed in a kind of succulent rutilant taffeta. The name, he was thinking: as artificial as the huge aureate wig. He said:

"I grant its cleverness. The name, I mean. I should imagine your real name is something like let me see Irma Polansky—no, wait, Edelmann, something like that." She looked very hard back at him.

"Do you read much poetry, professor?" Sperr Lansing asked.

"Well, I guess I hardly have the time these days." This Professor Balaglas flashed glasses in the lights. He had the soft face of a boy devoted to his mother and wore a hideous spotted bow tie. "What with working on the problems that this kind of movie under present discussion gives rise to." There was laughter. The audience was full of mouths always, as it were, at the ready, lips parted in potential ecstasy. "I have a collection of rock records like everybody else, of course. It's the job of poets to get close to the people. We shall be able to use poets in the new dispensation," he promised. "Rhymes are of considerable value in hypnopaedia or sleep-teaching. A great deal of the so-called poetry they write these days—"

"Who writes?" Enderby asked.

"I don't mean you, professor. I never read anything you wrote. You may be very clear and straightforward for all I know." Laughter. "I mean, you've been using very clear and straightforward language to me tonight." Very great laughter.

"The point I was trying to make," Enderby said. "About her name, that is." He shoulder-jerked towards the star. "There you see the poetic process exemplified in a small way.

Ermine—suggesting opulence, wealth, softness, luxury. Elderley—the piquancy of contrast with her evident near-youth, no longer *very* young, of course, but it happens to everybody, and the denotation of the name. The small *frisson* of gerontophilia."

Sperr Lansing did not seem to be greatly enjoying his job. He was a man adept at appearing to be on top of everything, ready with quip and *oeillade*, but the eyes now had become as glassy as those of a hung hare. "Get on top of whom?" he tried, and then saw he was being betrayed into unbecoming lowness. There was, rightly, no audience laugh.

Miss Elderley cunningly got in with "I used to know a poem about the wreck of something." There were relieved sniggers.

"The Hesperus perhaps," Professor Isinglass (?) brightly said.

"Naw, this went 'The boy stood on the burning deck—' "

A thing exquisitely coarse shot up from Enderby's schooldays. It was neat, too. Dirty verse depended upon an almost Augustan neatness. " 'The boy stood in the witness box,' " he recited, " 'Picking his nose like fury—' " There were loud cries of hey hey and Lansing picked up a packet of Shagbag or something from among the various commercial artifacts stowed behind the ashtray-and-waterbottle table. "I think," he cried, "it's time we heard another important message. Girls," he counter-recited, "is your fried chicken greasy?"

"—'Little blocks, And aimed it at the jury.' "

"Because if you want it to be crisp and dry as the bone within, here's how to do it." There were at once waving fat studio major-domos running around, and the monitor screens began to show hideous greasy fried chicken, oleic, aureate.

"All right all right," Sperr Lansing was saying, "it's going to be Jake Summers next. Look," he said to Enderby, "keep it clean, willya."

"I was only trying to keep it vulgar," Enderby said. "It's evidently a vulgar sort of show."

"It wasn't till you got on it, buster," Miss Elderley began.

"Well, damn it," Enderby said, "the amount of tit you're showing, if you don't mind my saying so, is hardly conducive to the maintenance of a high standard of intellectual discourse."

"You leave my bosoms out of this—"

"There's only *one* bosom. A bosom is a dual entity."

"I object to him using that word about me. I've met these bastards before—"

"I object to being called a bastard—"

"Either sex maniacs or fags—"

Sperr Lansing composed his face to beatific calm and told the camera and the audience: "Welcome back, folks. Now here's the man who pays for a moon shot with every Broadway success he writes. Somebody once said that there were only two men of the theatre—Jake Speare and Jake Summers. Well, here's one of them."

Underneath the applause and the shambling on of a small near-bald clerkly man in spectacles and sweatshirt, Enderby said to Miss Elderley:

"I suppose you wouldn't call that vulgar. Eh? Jakes Peare, indeed. And I'll tell you another thing—I won't be called a bloody fag."

"I didn't say that. I said the British are either fags or sex maniacs. Keep it quiet, willya."

For Sperr Lansing was now praising this Summers man lavishly to his face. "—five hundred and forty-five performances is what I have written down here. To what do you attribute—"

Summers was wearily modest. "Write well, I guess. Keep it clean, I guess. When they do it, they do it offstage." Applause and laughter. "No, yah. Let them hear about sex and violence, I guess, not see it." A and L. "Talking about poetry," he said, "I used to write it. Then I meet this guy on his yacht and he says give it up, there's nothing in it." Applause.

Enderby saw the tortured ecstatic face of Father Hopkins on top of the bugler and went mad. "Filth," he said, "filth and vulgarity."

"Aw, can it willya," Miss Elderley said. Professor Glass said:

"It is not my place, not here and now that is, to proffer any diagnosis of er Professor Endlessly's perpetual er manic state of excitation. Facts must be faced, though. The world has changed. England is no longer the centre of a world empire. The English language has found its finest er flowering in what he called a colonial territory."

"Attaboy," Miss Elderley said. "Wow."

"Be fair, I guess," Summers said. "Those boys with guitars."

"He feels his manhood threatened," Professor Elderglass went on. "Note how his dress proclaims an er long-dead national virility. He thinks man is being abolished. His kind of man."

"Bankside," Summers said. Everybody roared.

"Yes, the character or homunculus in your play. Man *qua* man. Man in his humanity. Man as Thou not It. Man as a person not a thing. These are not very helpful expressions, but they supply a clue. What is being abolished is autonomous man—the inner man, the homunculus, the possessing demon, the man defended by the literatures of freedom and dignity."

"That's it, you bastard," Enderby said, "you've summed it all up."

"His abolition has been long overdue. He has been constructed from our ignorance, and as our understanding increases, the very stuff of which he is composed vanishes. Science does not dehumanise man, it de-homunculises him, and it must do so if it is to prevent the abolition of the human species. Hamlet, in the play I have already mentioned, by your fellow-playwright, Mr. Summers, said of man, 'How like a god.' Pavlov said, 'How like a dog.' But that was a step forward. Man is much more than a dog, but like a dog he is within range of a scientific analysis."

"Look," shouted Enderby over the applause, "I won't have it, see. We're free and we're free to take our punishment. Like Hopkins. I suppose you'd watch him doing it with your bloody neat little bow tie on and say how like a dog. Well, he's been punished enough with this bloody film or movie as you'd call it, bloody childish. That's his hell. He was gall, he was heartburn."

"He should have taken Windkill," Jake Summers said and got roars. Enderby was very nearly sidetracked.

"Leave the commercials to me, Jake," Lansing said, delighted. "And talking about commercials it's time we took another—"

"Oh no it bloody well isn't," Enderby shouted. "You can keep your bloody homunculus, for that's all he is—"

"Pardon me, it's you who believe in the homunculus—"

"Man was always violent and always sinful and always will be."

"And now he's got to change."

"He won't change, not unless he becomes something else. Can't you see that that's where the drama of life is, the high purple, the tragic—"

"Oh my," Jake Summers sighed histrionically and was at once loudly rewarded. "No time for comedy," he added and then was not clearly understood.

"The evolution of a culture," Professor Lookingglass

said, "is a gigantic exercise in self-control. It is often said that a scientific view of man leads to wounded vanity, a sense of hopelessness, and nostalgia—"

"Nostalgia means homesickness," Enderby cried. "And we're all homesick. Homesick for sin and colour and drunkenness—"

"Ah, so that's what it is," Miss Elderley said. "You're stoned."

"Homesick for the past." Enderby could feel himself ready to weep. But then fire possessed him just as Sperr Lansing said, "And now we let our sponsor get a word in—" Enderby stood and declaimed:

*"For how to the heart's cheering*
*The down-dugged ground-hugged grey*
*Hovers off, the jay-blue heavens appearing*
*Of pied and peelèd May!"*

"Fellers," Sperr Lansing said, "do you ever feel, you know, not up to it?" He held in his hands a product called, apparently, Mansex. "Well, just watch this." Then he turned on Enderby, as did everybody, including the sweating studio major-domos. The band, which appeared to have a whole Wagnerian brass section as well as innumerable saxophones and a drummer in charge sitting high on a throne, gave out very piercingly and thuddingly.

*Blue-beating and hoary-glow height; or night, still higher,*
*With belled fire and the moth-soft Milky Way,*
*What by your measure is the heaven of desire,*
*The treasure never eyesight got, nor was ever guessed what for the hearing?*

SPERR: Well I don't think it can. You'd better get on to Harry right away.

ENDERBY: Fucking home uncle us (????) indeed. Ill give you fucking home uncle as (?????). Degradation of humanity. No, but it was not these the jading and jar of the cart (?) times tasking it is fathers (?) that asking for ease of the sodden with its sorrowing hart (art?) not danger electrical horror then further it finds the appealing of the passion is tenderer (?) in prayer apart other I gather in measure her minds burden in winds (????????)

# EIGHT

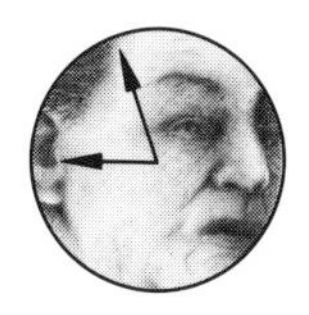

**AND** I'll tell you another thing," said the man in the bar. "Your queen of England. She owns half of Manhattan."

"That's a lie," Enderby said. "Not that I give a bugger either way."

It was a small dark and dirty bar not far from the television theatre whence Enderby had been not exactly ejected but as it were ushered with some measure of acrimony. The programme that had been recorded could not, it was felt, go out. The audience had been told too and had been angry until told that they were going to do it all over again but this time without Enderby.

"What's the matter with you then?" this man asked. "You not patriotic?" He had a face round and shiny as an apple but somehow unwholesome, as though a worm was burrowing within. "Your Winston Churchill was a great man, wasn't he? He wanted to fight the commies."

"He was half American," Enderby said, then sipped at his sweetish whisky sour.

"Ain't nothing wrong with that. You trying to say there's something wrong with that?"

"After six years of fighting the bloody Germans," Enderby said, "we were supposed to spend another six or sixty years fighting the bloody Russians. And he always had these big cigars when the rest of us couldn't get a single solitary fag."

"What's that about fags?"

"Cigarettes," Enderby explained. "While you've a lucifer to light your fag, smile, boys, that's the style."

"My mother was German. That makes me half German. You trying to say there's something wrong with that?" And then: "You one of these religious guys? What's that you was saying about Lucifer?"

"The light-bringer. Hence a match. For lighting a fag."

"I'd set a light to them. I'd burn the bastards. It's fags that pretends the downfall. The Sin of Sodom. You ever read that book?"

"I don't think so."

"Jack," this man called to the bartender, "do you have that book?"

"Gave it back to Shorty."

"There," the man said. "But there's plenty around. Where you going now?"

"No more money," Enderby said. "Just one subway token."

"Right. And your queen of England owns half the real estate in Queens. That's why they call it Queens, I guess."

Enderby walked slowly, not too displeased, towards the Times Square subway hellmouth. He had told the bastards anyway. Not apparently as many as he had expected to tell, but these matters could not always be approached quantitatively. He passed a great lighted pancake house and hungered as he did. No, watch diet, live. A whining vast black came out at him and whined for a coin. Enderby was able sincerely to say that he had no money, only a subway token. Well gimme that mane. I kin sell that for thirty cents. But how do I get home? That ain't ma problem mane. Enderby shook his head compassionately. Two other blacks and a white man, dispossessed or alienated, had made a little street band for their own apparent pleasure—guitar, flageolet, tambourine. Music of the people—was that a possible approach?

*An ole Sain Gus he said yo born in sin*
*Cos when Eve ate de apple she let de serpent in*

He shook his head sadly and went down below, wondering not for the first time whether it was really necessary to be so punctilious about setting the turnstile working with a token in the slot, since so many black and brown youths merely used, without official protest, the exit gate as an entrance. There were a lot of noisy ethnic people, as they were stupidly called, around, but Enderby did not fear. Nor was it just a matter of his being illegally armed. It was a matter of being *integer vitae* and also of having committed himself to a world in which pure and simple aggression was to be accepted as part of the human fabric. Die with Beethoven's Ninth howling and crashing away or live in a safe world of silly clockwork music?

He got into a train, thinking, and then realised his mistake. This was not the uptown express to 96th Street but the uptown local. Never mind. He was interested to see that, among the few passengers, all harmless, there was a nun. She was a nun of a kind not to be seen in backward Europe or North Africa, since she wore the new reformed habit, fruit of ill-thought-out Catholic liberalism. There had been a nun in a class he had taken in the previous semester, though it had been a long time before he realised it, since she wore a striped sailor sweater and bell-bottomed trousers. When he discovered her name was Sister Agnes, he had wondered if she were part of some religious mission to seawomen. But then she left the class, being apparently put off by Enderby's occasional blasphemies. This nun on the train was dressed in a short skirt that revealed veal-to-the-heel legs in what looked like lisle stockings, a modest tippet, a rather heavy pectoral cross, and the wimple of her order. She had a round shining Irish face with a dab of lipstick. Of the world and yet not of it. She had a Bloomingdale's shopping bag on her lap. She smiled at some small inner vision—perhaps of the kettle on the hob singing peace into her breast, a doorstep spiced veal sandwich waiting for her supper. Enderby looked kindly at her.

The two brown louts who got on, quickening Enderby's heart, spoke not Spanish but Portuguese. Brazilians, a new spice for the ethnic stew, plenty of Indian blood there. Enderby at once feared for the nun, but she seemed protected either by her reformed uniform or by their own superstition. They leered instead towards a blonde lay girl reading some thick college tome, probably on what was called sociology, further up the car. CRISTO 99. JISM 292. They wore long flared pants with goldish studs stretching on the outer seams from waist to instep. Their jackets were of a bolero type, blazoned with symbols of destruction and death—thunderbolt, rawhead, fasces, Union Jack, swastika. One of them wore a *Gott Mit Uns* belt. They stood, two brown left hands gently frotting the metal monkey pole. They spoke to each other. Enderby hungrily hearkened.

"*E conta o que ele fez com ela e tem fotografia e tudo.*"

"*Um velho lélé da cuca.*"

They were apparently talking about literature. At the next stop they grinned at everybody, leered at the girl with the tome, mock-genuflected at the nun, then got off. "*Bôa noite,*" Enderby said, having once had a regular drunk from Matosinhos in his Tangier bar, one much given in his cups to protesting the deuterocaroline dowry. Now there was a kind of quiet general exhalation. At the next stop but one three nice WASP boys, as Enderby took them to be, got on. In the eyes of two of them was the very green of the ocean between Plymouth and Plymouth Rock. The other had warm tea-hued pupils. They were chubby-faced and wore toggled duffel jackets.

Their hair belonged to some middle crinal zone between aseptic nord and latinindian jet-walled lousehouse. Without words and almost with the seriousness of asylum nurses they at once set upon an unsavoury-looking matron who began to cry out Mediterranean vocables of distress. Staggering but laughing, they had her staggering upright, held from the back by the tea-eyed one, while her skirt was yanked up to disclose sensible thick navy-blue knickers. One drew nail scissors and began delicately to slice at them. Oh my God, Enderby prayed. Gerontal violation. The nun, who had lapsed back into her dream of supper, was quicker than Enderby. She staggered onto them, the train jolting much, hitting with her Bloomingdale's bag. Delighted, the nail-scissored one turned on her, while the knicker-ripping was completed by hand by the others. Enderby was, in the desperate resigned second before his own intervention, interested to see the reading girl go on reading and even turn a page, while an old man slept uneasily and two black boys chewed and watched as if this were television. Enderby, tottering to the train's rocking, was now there with his stick. How much better to be out of it, the kettle on the hob, a spiced veal sandwich. Delighted, the nail-scissored one turned on him, dropping his nun to the deck to pray or something. And yet God has not said a word, nor they either. Yet noises were coming out, even out of Enderby, such as yaaark and grerrr and gheee.

"Scrot," one of them said. "Balzac." Educated then. You did not educate people out of aggression, great liberal fallacy that. The one with scissors was trying to stab at Enderby's crotch. The other two had left the matron to moan and stagger and were grinning at the prospect of doing in an old man. Enderby lunged out at random with his stick and, as he had expected, it was at once grasped—by, strangely, two left hands. Enderby pulled back. The sword emerged, half then wholly naked. They had not expected this. It flashed Elizabethanly in the swaying train, hard to keep upright, they all had legs bowed to it like sailors. Whitelady looked down amazed at Enderby from an EMPLOY A VETERAN advertisement. LOPEZ 95 MARLOWE 93 BONNY SWEET ROBIN 1601. Enderby at once pinked one of them in the throat and red spurted. "Glory be to God," the nun prayed, getting up from the deck. Spot-of-blood-and-foam dapple Bloom lights the orchard apple. Enderby tried a more ambitious thrust in some belly or other. It hit a belt. He tried underarm pricking on one who raised a fist wrapped round an object dull and hard. He drew a sword tip on which red rode and danced. And thicket and thorp are merry With silver-surféd cherry. The train danced clumsily to its next stop. There was a lot of loud language now—fuckabastardyafuckingpiggetyafuckingballs. One of the boys, the throat-pinked one who now gave out blood like a pelican, led the way out. Enderby thrust towards his backside and then felt pity. Enough was enough. He lunged halfheartedly instead at the one who had not yet received gladial attention. Ow ouch. Nothing really: plenty of flesh there: a fleshy-bottomed race. They were all out now, the oxter-pierced bleeding quite nastily, all crying bitterly and fiercely fuckfuckassbastardcuntingfuckbastardfuckingpig and so on. The door closed and their faces were execrating holes out there on the platform. The human condition. No art without aggression. Then they were execrating briefly out of the past into the future. Enderby, winded and dangerously palpitant, picked up his hollow stick from the deck, not without falling on his face first. He found his seat and, with great difficulty, threaded the trembling bloody metal back in. The matron sat very still, handbag on lap, blue at the lips, seeing visions that made her cry out. The reading girl turned another page. The old man slept uneasily. The two black boys, seated tailorwise, made fencing gestures wow sssh zheeeph and so on at each other. The nun, still standing, said:

"That's a terrible weapon you have there."

"Look," Enderby panted, "that was my stop. I've gone past my bloody stop."

"You can ride back from the next one."

"But I've no money." And then: "Are you all right now? Is she all right now?" They were all all right now except for the shock.

"You can get on without a token," the nun said. "A lot of them do it." And then: "You shouldn't be carrying a thing like that around with you. It's against the law."

"Entitled self-protection. Bugger the law."

"Are you an Englishman?" Nodnod. Nod. "I thought so from your way of swearing. Are you a Protestant?" Shake-shake. "I said to myself you had a Catholic face."

"Aren't you," Enderby said, "frightened? Travelling like this. A lot of thugs and rapists and—"

"I trust in Almighty God."

"He wasn't all that bloody quick in. Coming to your. Help."

"Are you all right now? You look very pale."

"Heart," Enderby said. "Heart."

"I'll say a decade of the rosary for you."

"You have your supper first. A nice veal sandwich. A cup of—"

"What a strange thing to say. I can't stand veal."

Enderby got shakily off at the next stop but would not take a free ride back to 96th Street. Timorousness? No, he did not think it was that. It was rather something to do with vital integrity, not lowering oneself, wearing a suit evocative of an age of decency when gentlemen thrashed niggers but paid their bills. So he walked as far as the Symphony movie house and thought it might be a good plan to sit there, resting in the dark, judging once more, if he had the strength, certain ethical aspects of *The Wreck of the Deutschland,* and then go home calmly and starving to bed. But, of course, approaching the paybox, he realised once more he had no money. He said, to the bored chewing black bespectacled girl behind the grille:

"Look, I just want to go in for a minute. I was involved in the making of this er movie, you see. Something I have to check. Business not pleasure." She did not seem to care. She waved him towards the cavern of the antechamber, see man in charge, man. But there was no one around who cared much. It was past the hour for anyone to care much. Enderby entered tempestuous darkness: the breakers were rolling on the beam of the *Deutschland* with ruinous shock. And canvas and compass, the whorl and the wheel idle for ever to waft her or wind her with, these she endured. There did not seem to be, now he could see better, many audients taking it all in. An old man slept uneasily. Some blacks chortled inexplicably at the sight of one stirring from the rigging to save the wild womankind below, with a rope's end round the man, handy and brave. Some fine swooping camerawork showed him being pitched to his death at a blow, for all his dreadnought breast and braids of thew. Cut to night roaring, with the heartbreak hearings a heartbroke rabble, the woman's wailing, the crying of child without check. Then a lioness arose breasting the babble. Gertrude, lily, Franciscan robe already rent, spoke of courage, God. Then came the flashback —*Deutschland,* double a desperate name. Beautifully contrived colour contrasts: black uniforms, white nun flesh, red yelling gob, blood, a patch of yellow convent-garden daffodils crushed under black-booted foot. Hitler appeared briefly, roaring something (beast of the waste wood) to black approbation in the audience.

Away in the loveable west, on a pastoral forehead of Wales, Father Tom Hopkins, S.J., seemed mystically or ESPishly aware of something terrible going on out there somewhere. Putting down his breviary, he dreamed back to boy-and-girl love. A student in Germany, Gertrude not yet coifed, passion amid *Vogelgesang* in the Schwarzwald. Rather touching, really, but far too naked. Song of Hitlerjugend marching in the distance. Bad times coming for us all. Ja ja, Tom. It all seemed pretty harmless, Enderby thought. It aroused desire to see off the Nazis, no more, but that had already been done, Enderby vaguely assisting. And so he left. He walked down chill blowing Broadway as far as 91st Street, then crossed towards Columbus Avenue. At this point.

At this point it happened again. Pain was pumped rapidly into his chest and he stopped breathing. The surplus of pain overflowed into the left shoulder and went rattling down the arm to the elbow. At the same time both legs went suddenly dead and the tough metalled stick was not enough to sustain him. He went over gently onto the sidewalk and lay, writhing, trying to deal with the pain and the inability to breathe like a pair of messages that both had to be answered at once. Pain passed and breath shot in with the hiss of an airtight can being opened. But still he lay, now feeling the cold. A few people passed by, naturally ignoring him, some junky, a man knifed, dangerous to be involved. And they were right, of course, in a world that thought the worst of involvement. Why did you help him, mister? Got scared, did you? Let's see what you got in your pockets. What's this? A stomach tablet? That's a laaaugh. Soon he was able to get up. Blood and a kind of healthy pain were flowing into his legs. He felt all right, even gently elated. After all, he knew now where he stood. There was no need to plan anything long—that Odontiad, for instance. A loosening artistic obligation.

There was only the obligation of setting things in order. He might live a long time yet, but time would be doled out to him in very small denominations, like pocket money. On the other hand, there was no need to work at living a long time. He had not done too badly. He was fifty-six, already had done four years better than Shakespeare. As for poor Gervase Whitelady. Kindly he suddenly decided to allow Whitelady to live till 1637, which meant he could benefit from the critical acumen of Ben Jonson.

He got to the apartment block without difficulty. Mr. Audley, the black guard, sat in his chair in the warmth of the foyer, while the many telescreens showed dull programmes—people muffled up hurrying round the corner, the basement empty, the main porch newly free of entering Enderby. They nodded at each other, Enderby was allowed in, he took the elevator to his floor, he entered his apartment. Thanked, so to speak, Almighty God. He drew his bloody sword and executed a courtly flourish with it at the mess in the kitchen. Then he cleaned off the blood with a dishrag. His stomach, crassly ignoring the day's circulatory warnings, growled at him, knowing it was in the kitchen, messy or not.

There was an episode, Enderby remembered, in Galsworthy's terrible Forsyte or Forsyth epic, in which some old scoundrel of the dynasty faced ruin and determined to kill himself like a gentleman by eating a damn good dinner. In full fig, by George. By George, they had got him an oyster. By George, he had forgotten to put his teeth in, and here was a brace of mutton chops grilled to a turn. A rather repulsive story, but it did not debar Galsworthy from getting the Order of Merit and the Nobel Prize. Enderby had never got or gotten anything, not even the Heinemann Award for Poetry, but he did not give a bugger. He did not now propose to eat himself to death, in a subforsytian manner befitting his station, but rather just not to give a bugger. To take a fairly substantial supper with, since time might be short, a few unwonted luxuries added. Such as that French chocolate ice cream that was iron-hard in the deep freeze. And that small tin of pâté mixed in the great culminatory stew he envisaged after, for tidiness' sake, finishing off his Sara Lee collection and eating the potato pieces and spongemeat that waited for a second chance, nestling ready in their fat. And to get through the mixed pickles and Major Gray's chutney. He had always hated waste.

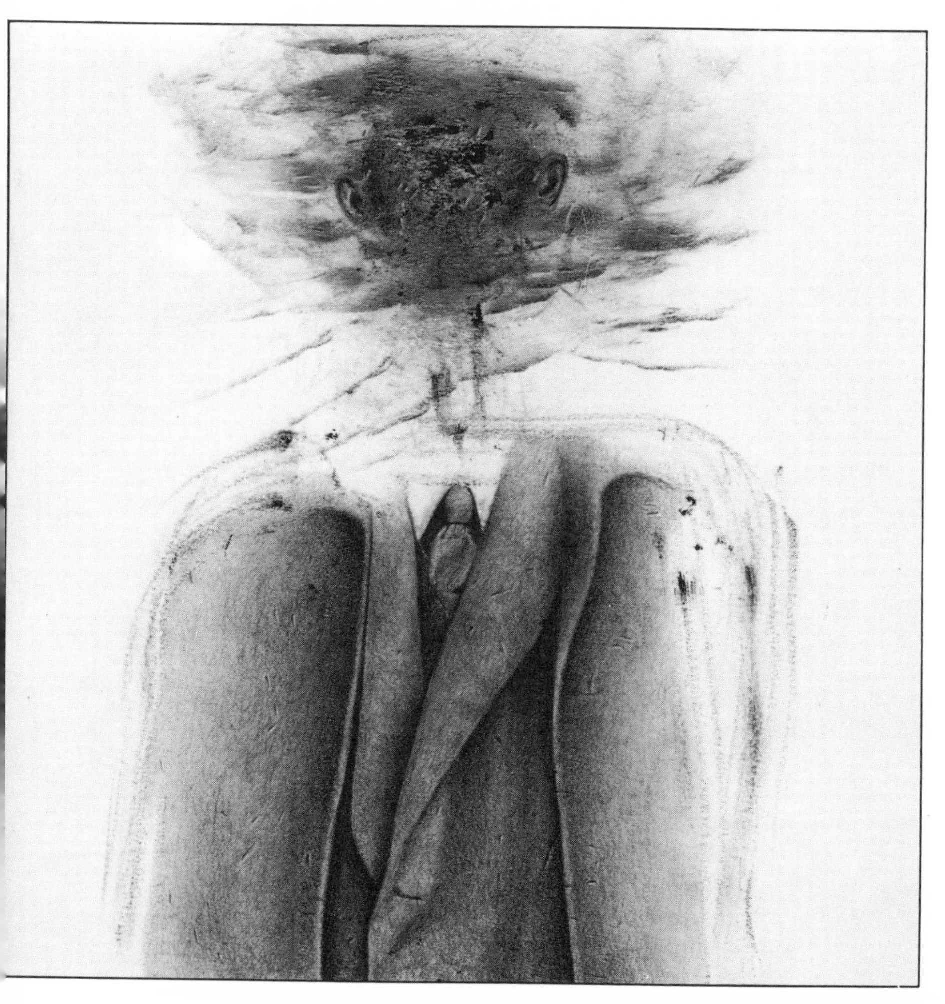

# NINE

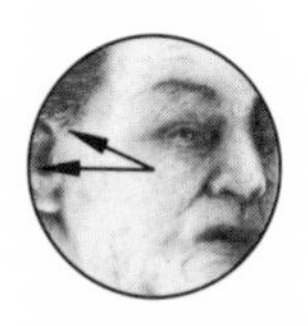

**ENDERBY'S** supper was interrupted by two telephone calls. During the stew course (two cans of corned beef, frozen onion rings, canned carrots, a large Chunky turkey soup, pâté, a dollop of whisky, Lea and Perrin's, pickled cauliflowers, the remains of the spongemeat and the crinkle-cut potato bits) Ms. Tietjens sobbed to him briefly without preamble: I'm sick, I tell ya, I'm all knotted up inside, I'm sick, sick, there's something wrong with me, I tell ya; and Lloyd Utterage confirmed the impending fulfilment of his threat, so that Enderby was constrained to tell him to come along and welcome, black bastard, and have an already bloody sword stuck into his black guts. Enderby placidly ended his meal with the French ice cream (brought to near melting in a saucepan over a brisk flame) with raspberry jam spread liberally over, spooning the treat in on rich tea biscuits he ate as he spooned. Then he had some strong tea (six Lipton's bags in the pint ALABAMA mug) and lighted up a White Owl. He felt pretty good, as they said in American fiction, though distended. All he needed now, as again they would say in American fiction, and he laughed at the conceit, was a woman.

A woman came while he was making himself more tea. He was surprised to hear the doorbell ring with no anterior warning on the intercommunication system from the black guard below. Every visitor was supposed to be screened, frisked, reported to the intended visited before actually appearing. The woman at the door was young and very attractive in a reactionary way, being dressed in a bourgeois grey costume with a sort of nutria or coypu or something coat swinging open over it. She wore over decently arranged chastaigne hair a little pillbox hat of the same fur. She was carrying a handful of slim volumes. She said:

"Mr. Enderby?"

"Or Professor, according to the nature of. How did you get here? You're not supposed just to come up, you know, without a premonition."

"A what?"

"A forewarning from the gunman."

"Oh. Well, I said it was a late visit from one of your students and that you were expecting me. It *is* all right, isn't it?"

"Are you one of my students?" Enderby asked. "I don't seem to—"

"I am in a sense. I've studied your work. I'm Dr. Greaving."

"Doctor?"

"From Goldengrove College."

"Oh very well then, perhaps you'd better. That is to say." And he motioned courtlily that she should enter. She entered, sniffing. "Just been cooking," Enderby said. "My supper, that is to say. Can I perhaps offer?"

In the sitting room there was a small table. Dr. Greaving put down her books on it and at once sat on the straight-backed uncomfortable chair nearby.

"Whisky or something like that?"

"Water." Now in, she had become vaguely hostile. She looked up thinly at him.

"Oh, very well. Water." And Enderby went to get it. He let the faucet run but the stream did not noticeably cool. He brought some back warmish and put the glass down with care next to the slim volumes. He saw they were of his own work. British editions, American not existing. "Oh," he said. "How did you manage to get hold of those?"

"Paid for them. Ordered them through a Canadian bookseller. When I was in Montreal." Enderby now noticed that she had taken out of her handbag a small automatic pistol, a lady killer.

"Oh," he said. "Now perhaps you'll understand why they're so keen down below on checking visitors and so on. Why have you brought that? It seems, to say the least, unnecessary." He marvelled at himself saying this. (Cinna the poet: tear him for his bad verses?)

"You deserve," she said, "to be punished. Incidentally, my name is *not* Dr. Greaving. But what I said about being a student of your work is true."

"Are you Canadian?" Enderby asked.

"You seem to be a big man for irrelevancies. One thing you're a big man in." She drank some water, keeping her eyes on him. The eyes were of a kind of triple-sec colour. "You'd better bring a chair."

"There's one in the kitchen," Enderby said with relief. "I'll just go and—"

"Oh no. No dashing into the kitchen to the telephone. If you tried that anyway I'd come and shoot you in the back. Get that chair over there." It was not really a chair. It was a sort of very frail Indian-style coffee table. Enderby said:

"It's really a sort of very frail. It belongs to my landlady. I might." He was really, to his surprise, quite enjoying this. It seemed quite certain to him now that he was not going to die of cancer of the lung.

"Bring it. Sit on it." He did. He sat on its edge, pity to damage so frail a, horrible though he had always thought it. He said:

"Now what I can do for you, Miss er?"

"I'm not," she said, "going to tolerate any more of this persecution. And it's Mrs., as you perfectly well know. Not that I'm living with him any more, but that's another irrelevance. I'm not going to have you," she said, "getting into my brain."

Enderby gaped. "How?" he said. "What?"

"I know them by heart," she said, "a great number of them. Well, I don't want it any more. I want to be free. I want to get on with my own things, can't you see that, you bastard?" She pointed the little gun very steadily at Enderby.

"I don't understand," Enderby said. "You've read my things, you say. That's what they're for, to be read. But there's no er compulsion to read them, you know."

"There's a lot of things there's no compulsion for. Like going to the movies to see a movie that turns out to be corruptive. But then you're corrupted, just the same. You never know in advance." As this seemed to her ears apparently, as certainly to his, to be a piece of neutral or even friendly expository talk, she added sharply, with a gun gesture, "You bastard."

"Well, what do you want me to do?" Enderby asked. "Unwrite the damned things?" And then, this just striking him, "You're mad, you know, you must be. Sane readers of my poems don't—"

"That's what they all say. That's what *he* said, till I stopped him."

"How did you stop him?" Enderby asked, fascinated.

"Another irrelevance. Don't you bastards ever think of your responsibility?"

"To our art," Enderby said. "Oh my God," he added in quite impersonal distress, "do you mean there's to be no more art? Aye, by St. Anne," he added, seeing that *mad* was a very difficult term to define, "and ginger shall be hot in the—"

"There you go again. Decent people suffer and you sit on your fat ass talking about *art*."

"That's just low abuse," he frowned. "Besides, I don't

think you could call this really sitting." She had, he could see, beneath the peel of the mad hate, a sweet face, a Catholic face, ruined, God help the girl, ruined. "No, no," he said in haste. "Relevance is what is called for. I see that." And then: "Look. If you shoot me, it won't make any difference, will it? It won't destroy the words I wrote." And then: "What intrigues me, if that doesn't sound too irrelevant a term, is how you got to know them in the first place. My poems, I mean. I mean, not many people do. And here you are, young as I see, also beautiful if I may say that without sounding frivolous or irrelevant, knowing them. If you do know them, that is, of course, I mean," he ended cunningly.

"Oh, I know them all right," she cried scornfully. "I see lines set up at eye level in the subway. There's one in fifteen-foot-high Gothic letters just by the Port Authority. They get sort of stitched into that Times Square news-ticker thing."

"Interesting," Enderby said.

"There you go," she gun-pointed. "*Interesting*. So tied up in yourself and your so-called work you're just *interested*. *Interested* in how it happened, and all that crap about youth and beauty and the other irrelevancies."

"They're not irrelevant," Enderby said sharply. "I won't have that. Beauty and youth are the only things worth having. Dust hath closed Helen's eye. And they go. And here you are, saying they don't matter. Silly bitch," he attempted, not sure whether that would pull the trigger.

"That bastard introduced me to them, if you must know," she said, not listening. "It started off when we were on our honeymoon and it was in the morning and he giggled and said The marriage contract was designed in spite of what the notaries think to be by only one pen signed and that is mine and full of ink. But he didn't, oh no, just giggled."

"A mere jeu d'esprit," Enderby mumbled regretfully, remembering his own honeymoon when he didn't either, just giggled.

"That's how that bastard started me off. Anything to make me suffer, bastard as he was."

"That doesn't sound like a North American idiom," Enderby said in wonder. "That's more the way they speak where I come from."

"Yes. Possession, isn't it? Takeover. *Bastard*."

"Well, blame him, not me. I mean, damn it, it could have been William Shakespeare, couldn't it? Or Robert Bridges, bloody fool, not worthy of him. *And thy loved legacy, Gerard, hath lain Coy in my breast*. Bloody evil idiot. Or Geoffrey Grigson."

"Shakespeare's dead," she said reasonably. "So may the other two be, whoever they are. But you're alive. You're here. I've waited a long time for this."

"How did you know I was here?"

"Irrelevant irrelevant. It was announced, if you must know, after a talk show this evening that you were going to be on tomorrow night."

"Recorded it too early. Take too much for granted. I'm not. It's all been changed now."

"And I called them and they said you wouldn't be on and they'd never have you on. But they gave me your address."

"The swine. They're not supposed to. Address a private thing. Sheer bloody vindictiveness." He fumed briefly. She smiled thinly in scorn and said:

"Self self self. Self and art. You bastard."

"Oh," Enderby said, "get the bloody shooting over with. We've all got to die sometime. You too. They'll send you to the chair, or whatever barbarity they have now. I don't believe in capital punishment. I cancelled this long poem about Pelagius. I won't write the Odontiad. I've nothing on hand. Come on, get it over."

"Oh no. Oh no. Oh no. What you're going to do is to grovel. And after that I may or I may not—"

"May not what?"

"You're not going to have a nice easy martyrdom. I know men. You'll be glad to grovel."

"Grovel grovel grovel," Enderby growled like a tom turkey. "Artists are expected to grovel, aren't they? While the charlatans and the plagiarists and the corrupters and the defilers and the politicians have their arseholes licked. What do you want me to do—*eat* the bloody things? I've just had supper, remember. And," cunningly, "you won't want to turn me into Jesus Christ, will you?"

"Blasphemous bastard."

"And, moreover, if I may say so, I don't see how you're going to *make* me grovel. Your only alternative is to use that bloody thing there. Well, I don't mind dying."

"Of course you don't. Enderby flopped over his slim volumes, blood coming out of his mouth. Not that that would ever get into books. I'd make sure of that. There are no martyrs these days. Except blacks."

"All right, then. I'm going to get up now, this bloody thing's uncomfortable anyway, and walk into that kitchen there, and get the block guard on the blower, tell him to bring the cops along." *Cops* was the only possible word, a *thriller* word. Okay buster you call the cops.

She kept shaking her head all the time. "Glad to grovel, glad to. I've seen it before. With him. I have six rounds in here. I'm a good shot, my father taught me, my father, worth ten of you, you bastard. I can nip at bits of you. Nip nip nip. Make you deaf. Make you noseless. Give you a fucking anatomical excuse for being sexless."

"Where did you get that idea from? Who taught you that? Who's been talking—"

"Irrelevant."

"Look," Enderby said, wondering whether, to be on the safe side, to make a good act of contrition or not. "I'm getting up." He got up. "That's better. And I'm going to go, as I said I would, to—"

"You won't make it, friend. Your anklebone will be shattered."

He realised bitterly that he did not want his anklebone shattered. Good clean death, yes. Altogether different, by George. "Well, then," he said. And then: "They'll come up, in. Pistol shots. Break the door down."

"Do you honestly believe that, you innocent bastard of an idiot? This is not safe little England. Do you honestly think that anyone would care?" She shook her head at his lack of cisatlantic sophistication. "Listen, idiot. Listen, bastard."

Enderby listened. Of course, yes. You got used to it in time. In time it was just a decoration of the silence. Silence in a baroque frame. I say, that's good, I could use that. He heard the whining of police cars and the scream of ambulances. And then, from the west, bang bang. Yes, of course.

"But," she said, "we'll make sure, won't we? Go over there and turn on the TV. Turn it on *loud*. Keep going round the dial till I tell you to stop." Enderby moved with nonchalance, but only to sit down on a *pouffe*. Much much better. He said, with nonchalance:

"You do it. Play Russian roulette with it. That's Nabokov," he said in haste, "not me. *Pale Fire*," he clarified.

"Bastard," she said. But she got up and walked towards him, pointing her little gun. It was a nice little weapon from the look of it. She had delightful legs, Enderby saw regretfully, and seemed to be wearing stockings, not those panty-hose abominations. Suspenders, what they called garters here, and then knickers. He was surprised to find himself, under the thick hot Edwardian trousers, responding solidly to the very terms. Camiknicks. Beyond his *pouffe*, she moved sidelong to the television set. She then switched on and turned the dial click click click with her left hand, looking towards Enderby and pointing her weapon. Enderby sat on his *pouffe* calmly, hands about his knees. She had been drawn now into a harmless area of entertainment. It was sound she was choosing, she would be in charge of the visual part. A new kind of art really, pop and audience participation and so on, gestures of creative impotence. There was a swift diachronic kaleidoscope of images and a quite interesting synthetic statement: Thats it I guess its quality for you and for your so send fifteen dollars only its Butch you love isnt it I guess so emphatic denial issued by. Then she came to a palpable war film and, eyes uninterested still, turned up the noise of bombardment. Enderby said:

"That's much too loud. The neighbours will complain."

"What?" She hadn't heard him. "Now," coming towards him, pointing. Enderby could see, in black and white, brave GIs in foxholes. Then grenades were thrown lavishly by the undersized enemy. "Take your clothes off."

"*What?*"

"Everything off. I want to see you in your horrible potbellied hairy filthy nakedness."

"How do you know it's—" And then: "Why?"

"Degradation. The first phase."

"No. Ow." She had fired the little gun but it had not hit Enderby. It had merely whistled past him at very nearly ear level. He saw her there, a kind of numinous blue smoke before her, and smelt what seemed rather appetising smoked bacon. And thus he faced the breakfast of his death. He turned his head to see that the spine of a large illustrated volume on his landlady's shelves now looked disfigured. It was called *Woman's Bondage*. He had dipped into it once—a very humourless book, not about sex after all. She had timed the firing very felicitously, as though she knew the war film by heart. A village had gone up very loudly into the air. But now there was a love scene between a GI and a woman in a nurse's uniform, her hair crisp in a wartime style.

"Go on. Take them off."

Enderby was wearing neither jacket nor tie. It was, of course, very hot. He was, God knew, often enough naked in here, but he was damned if he was going to be told to be naked.

"Go on. Now." And she prepared to aim.

"It is, after all, quite— I mean, I meant to do this anyway. I normally do, you see. But I'm doing it because I want to. Do you understand that?"

"Go on."

Enderby took off his waistcoat and then his shirt. He smelt his axillary fear very clearly.

"Go on."

"Oh dear," Enderby said with mock-humorous exasperation. "You are a hard little taskmistress."

"I've not even started yet. Go on."

In socks and underpants Enderby said: "Will that do?"

"Argh. Disgusting."

"Well, if I'm disgusting why do you want to—"

"Go on. To the horrible disgusting limit."

"No. Ow."

There was an ugly violet glass vase on the mantelpiece. She hit it very neatly as thunderous strafing was resumed on the screen. But at once a commercial break broke in. In unnatural high colour a smirking naked-shouldered woman made love to her slowly floating hair. Weave a circle round him, girls. No, not that. They wouldn't have the bloody sense. Sighing, Enderby stripped down to the limit. His phallus too palpably announced its interest in that camiknick business. He was, as they had so often told him in critical reviews, very much a belated man of the thirties. Sonnet form and so on. The television screen homed to fried chicken. Enderby hid the thing with his hands.

"Disgusting."

"Well, it was your idea, not mine."

"Now," she ordered. "You're going to piss on your own poems."

"*I'm going to what?*"

"Urinate. Micturate. Squirt your own filthy water on your own filthy poems. Go *on*."

"They're not filthy. They're clean. What stupid fucking irony. All the genuinely filthy pseudo-art and not-art that's about, and you pick on honest and clean and craftsmanlike endeavour—"

The weapon (in thrillerish locution: Enderby saw the word in botched print at the very moment of firing) spoke again. That frail Indian-type table thing proved itself very frail, tumbling over as though fist-hit in aesthetic viciousness. Enderby's phallus rose a few more notches. He said: "That's three. That means only three left."

"It's enough. Next time I promise it's going to be some of that ugly filthy fat hairy blubbery bloated—" She spoke out of smoke.

Enderby took up the top book with his right hand, his left hand still serving pudeur. It was *Fish and Heroes*, he saw tenderly. He couldn't open it one-handed, so he turned his bottom towards her and gave both hands to leafing the few but thickish leaves. By God what a genius he had then.

Wachet auf! *A fretful dunghill cock*
*Flinted the noisy beacons through the shires.*
*A martin's nest clogged the cathedral clock.*
*Still, it was morning. Birds could not be liars . . .*

And what would Luther have done in these circumstances? He was a great one for farting and shitting, but only on the Fiend. Piss on that Bible, Luther. Unthinkable. But then (O my God, poem there to be written, meaning have to live?) he might have thought: only a copy, the Book subsists above the single copy, I must live, spread the Word, the mature man gives in occasionally to the foolish, evil, mad. Luther lifted up his great skirts, disclosing a fierce red thursday, and pissed vigorously on a mere mess of Gothic print. Here stand I, I can in no wise do otherwise. Enderby said loudly:

"No!"

"I can see what you're looking at," she said. "That sonnet about the Reformation." She knew the bloody book so well, it seemed such a pity. The television film showed a whining GI, cap tucked in epaulette, whining: "Can't we talk this thing over, Mary?"

"Oh, all right then," Enderby said wearily. And he turned his nozzle, with some slight muscular effort, onto the page. "See," he said. "I'm doing my best. But nothing will come. It stands to reason nothing will come. *Stand*, blast you, is the operative word."

And then, Luther throwing, but it was an inkpot, they showed you the inkstained wall in Wittenberg, Enderby threw the book, which fluttered vogelwise, towards her. Instinctively she shot at it. He had known, somehow, she would. He strode, heavily naked, balls aswing, weapon pointing, through the smoke and the echo of noise. And yet God has not said a word. She aimed straight at him, saying, "If you think you're going to be a fucking martyr for art—"

"Said that already," Enderby said, and he grasped her wrist at the very instant of her firing vaguely at the ceiling. The noise and smell were surely excessive. He had that damned gun now, a dainty hot little engine. She clawed at his buttocks as he went to the window partly open for the heat. Threw the bloody thing out. "There," he said. Luther, he remembered for some reason, had married a nun. Christ's lily and beast of the waste wood. This girl now beat at him with teeny fists. Enderby had had a good supper. He saw the two of them in the little mirror above a bookshelf devoted to psychology deeply Jewish and anguished. He had his glasses on, he observed, would not indeed have been able to observe otherwise, otherwise, of course, naked. He gave her a push somewhere around the midriff. She ended up crying on a *pouffe*.

"Bastard bastard."

Enderby took off his glasses and placed them carefully on top of the television set, which, well into the noise of impending victory, he clicked off. "You and your bloody guns," he said. "Get you into a bloody mediaeval monastery full of great ballocky monks, that would teach you. Flabby, indeed. Blubber, for Christ's sake. Silenus, Falstaff." This was for his own benefit. "Think of those, blast you." His heart seemed to be pumping away very healthily. Noise of impending victory. Not with a whimper but. "Blaming me, indeed. Blaming poor dead Hopkins. As though I held the nuns down for them."

"Go away. Get away from me."

"I live here," Enderby said. "Sort of." And then he pulled, two-handed, at the hems. Cry, clutching heaven by the. That was just to get a rhyme with *Thames*. Rhine refused them, Thames would ruin them. Francis Thompson a far inferior poet. Hopkins appeared an instant, open-mouthed, clearly seen moaning at another's sin, though in the dark of the confessional. "You did it," Enderby said. "So fagged, so fashed, indeed. Get away for a bit, can't you?" Hopkins became a pale daguerreotype, then was washed completely out.

The skirt was elasticated at the waist and pulled down with little difficulty. In joy, Enderby saw the tops of stockings, suspenders, peach knickers.

"You filthy fucking—"

"Oh, this is all too American," Enderby said. "Sex and violence. What angel of regeneration sent you here?" For there was no question of mumbling and begging now. *Enderbius triumphans, exultans.*

# TEN

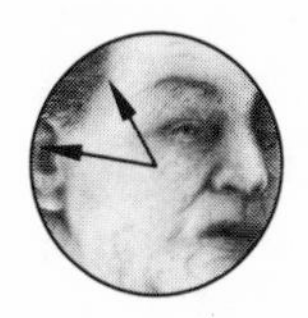

**THIS** third heart attack, if that was what it had really been, did not seem to be really all that bad—a mere sketch, as to remind him of its shape. But he knew its shape intimately already, that of a Spenglerian parabola. Yet another interpretation seemed, as he sat in the toilet and excreted as quietly as he could, there being a guest in the apartment, possible, though he was fain to reject it. An inner hand showing in delicate deadly gesture the impending chop or noose. He was glad in a way that she had taken possession of the circular bed, no room for him, since bed was a place where people frequently died, sometimes in their sleep. She lay naked on her back, telling, say, ten-twenty with her arms and seven-thirty with her legs, her delicate snoring indicating that it was a fine February night and all was well. She had left her home in Poughkeepsie, it appeared, and was obviously welcome to stay here with Enderby so long as she did not go out to buy another gun. She at least knew his work. Anyway, there was no question of thinking in terms of a nice long future. These heart attacks had been as good to Enderby as a *like* and *you know* harangue from one of his students. But he did not really want the chop to come tonight and in his sleep. He fancied doing some more vigorous death-dodging in the light. There was this to be said for New York: it was not dull.

Wiped and having flushed, Enderby went out to the kitchen to make tea. There would be a hell of a row tomorrow, today that was, when that dusky bitch Priscilla came to do the chores (How come an educated man like you live in such Gadarene filth—she was, after all, a Bible scholar); but there always was a hell of a row. This time there would probably be something about fornication and Cozbi as well as dirt. Enderby ate pensively a little cold left-over stew while he waited for the water to boil: quite delicious, really. He seemed to have lost a fair amount of protein in the last few hours, perhaps cholesterol too. When the tea had sufficiently brewed or drawn (five bags only; not overtempt Providence) and had been sharply sweetened and embrowned, he took it into the living room. He piled *pouffe* on *pouffe* to make himself comfortable in order to watch for the dawn to come up. He switched on the television set, which gave him a silly film apt for these small hours. It was a college musical of the thirties (*How come that such a scholar/Can put up with such squalor?/Just gimme hafe a dollar/And I'll make it spick and span, man.* There was a coincidence!) but it was made piquant with girls in peach-looking camiknicks with metallic hairdos. Enderby did some random leafing through the slim volumes she had brought for him to defile. God, what a genius, etc. The film, with interludes of advertising suspiciously cheap albums of popular music, went harmlessly on while he sipped his tea and browsed.

*You went that way as you always said you would,*
*Contending over the cheerful cups that good*
*Was in the here-and-now, in, in fact, the cheerful*
*Cups and not in some remotish sphere full*
*Of twangling saints, the-pie-in-the-sky-when-you-die*
*Of Engels as much as angels, whereupon I . . .*

He could not well remember having written that. Besides, the type was blurring. He saw without surprise that the film had changed to one, in very good colour too, about Augustine and Pelagius. Thank God. The thing had after all been at last artistically dealt with, no need after all for him to worry about finding an appropriate poetic form.

35. (SAY) EXTERIOR DAY A ROAD
*A man vigorously whipping his donkey, which brays in great pain. His wife comes along to tell him to desist.*

WIFE: Desist, desist. The poor creature meant no harm, Fabricius.

MAN: Farted in my face, didn't it? A great noseful of foul air.
(*he continues beating*)

WIFE: Foul, you say? She eats only sweet grass and fresh-smelling herbs, while you—you guzzle sour horsemeat and get drunk on cheap wine.

MAN: Oh, I do, do I? Take that, you slut.
(*he beats her till she bleeds*)

36. THE SAME TWO SHOT
*Pelagius and Obtrincius are watching. The noise and the cries are pitiable.*

OBTRINCIUS: What think you of that, O man of the northern seas? Evil, yes? It comes of the primal fetor of Adam which imbrues the world.

PELAGIUS: Ah no, my dear friend. Adam's sin was his own sin. It was not inherited by the generality of mankind.

OBTRINCIUS: But this is surely foul heresy! Why was Christ crucified except to pay, in Godflesh whose value is incomputable, for the Adamic sin we all carry? Have a care, my friend. There may be a bishop about listening.

PELAGIUS: Ah no, he came to show us the way. To teach us love. *Be ye perfect*, he said. He taught us that we are perfectible. That what you call evil is no more than ignorance of the way. Hi, you, my friend.

37. RESUME 35.
*The man Fabricius has now turned on his son, who, having apparently intervened to save his mother from the vicious blows, is bloody and bowed. The mother weeps bloodily. The ass looks on, sore but impassive, also bloody.*

MAN:

(*temporarily desisting*)

Huh? You address me, sir?

38. RESUME 36.

PELAGIUS:

(*cheerfully*)

Yes, my good man and brother in Christ.
*He moves out of the shot and into:*

39. TWO SHOT: MAN AND PELAGIUS

PELAGIUS: Ah, my poor friend, you have much to learn. Sweet reason has temporarily deserted you. Take breath and then blow out your anger with it. It is a mere ghost, a phantasm, totally insubstantial.

MAN: You use fine words, sir. But try using sweet reason to stop a donkey farting in your nose.

PELAGIUS: You should keep your nose away from the er animal's posterior. Sweet reason must surely tell you that.

MAN: Oh, well, mayhap you're right, sir. Anger wastes time and uses up energy. Come, wife. Come, son. I will be reasonable, God forgive me.

(*sketching a blessing, Pelagius moves out of shot*)

Sweet reason, my ass.

40. EXTERIOR DAY ROME: A SCENE OF UNBRIDLED REVELRY

*A LS of a sort of carnival. Instruments of the fifth century* A.D. *are blaring and thumping, while unbridled revellers frisk about, kissing and drinking and lifting kirtles.*

41. THE SAME GROUP SHOT

*A group of gorgers are greasily fingering smoking haunches and swineshanks, stuffing it in, occasionally vomiting it out.*

PELAGIUS (OS): My friends!
*They all look in the same direction, open mouths exhibiting half-chewed greasy protein.*

42. THEIR POV: PELAGIUS
*He stands with pilgrim's staff, looking with calm sorrow.*

PELAGIUS: Does not reason tell you that such excess is unreasonable? It coarsens the soul and harms the body.

(*There is a noise of lavish vomiting*)

There, you see what I mean.

43. PELAGIUS'S POV
*The gorgers look somewhat abashed, but a bold fat bald one speaks up baldly and boldly.*

FAT GORGER: We cannot help it, man of God, whoever you are, a stranger by your manner of speech. The seven deadly sins, of which gluttony, as thou mayhap knowest, is one, are the seven worms in the apple we ate at the great original feast which still goes on, and of which Adam and Eve are the host and the hostess.

ANOTHER GORGER:

(*much thinner, as with a worm, or even seven, inside him*)

Aye, he speaketh truly, monk, whoever thou art. We are born into sin through none of our willing, and has not Christ atoned for our sins, past, future, and to come?

44. RESUME 42.
PELAGIUS:

(*very loudly*)

No He Has Not.

45. A GROUP OF FORNICATORS
*Mitred bishops, bearded, venerable, lusty, look up from clipping their well-favoured whores. They look at each other, frown.*

46. INTERIOR NIGHT THE HOUSE OF FLACCUS
*The bishop Augustine sits at the end of dinner with his friend Flaccus, a public administrator. There are other guests, including Bishop Tarminius—one of the bishops who frowned in Scene 45.*

FLACCUS:

*(while a slave proffers a dish)*

Perhaps an apple, my lord bishop?

AUGUSTINE:

*(shuddering)*

Ah no, Flaccus my friend. If you only knew what part apples have played in my life—

TARMINIUS: And one apple in the life of all mankind.

AUGUSTINE:

*(looking at him for an instant, then nodding gravely)*

Yes, Tarminius, very true. But oh, the moonwashed apples of wonder in the neighbour orchard. I did not steal the apples because I needed them—indeed, my father's apples were far better, sweeter, rosier. I stole them because I wished to steal. To sin. It was my sin I loved, God help me.

FLACCUS: Aye, it is in all of us. Baptism is but a token of extinguishing the fire—

AUGUSTINE: Burning burning burning burning—

FLACCUS: But Christ paid, atoned, still makes the impact of our daily sin on the godhead less acute.

AUGUSTINE: Beware of theology, Flaccus. These deep matters have driven mad many a young brain.

TARMINIUS: You speak very true, Augustine. There is a man from Britain in our midst—didst know that?

AUGUSTINE: There are many from Britain in our midst—that misty northern island where the damp clogs men's brains. They are harmless enough. They blink in our southern light. They go down with the sun.

*(laughter)*

TARMINIUS: I refer to one, Augustine, who seems not to be harmless, whose gaze is very steady, who is impervious to sunstroke. His name is Pelagius.

FLACCUS:

*(frowning)*

Pelagius? That is not a British name.

TARMINIUS: His true name is Morgan, which, in their tongue, means man of the sea. Pelagius, in Greek, means exactly the—

AUGUSTINE:

*(testily)*

Yes yes, Tarminius. I think we all know what it means. Hm. I have heard a little about this man—a wandering friar, is he not? He has been exhorting the people to be kind to their wives and asses and warning of the dangers of gluttony. Also, I understand—

*(he looks sternly at Tarminius, who looks sheepish rather than shepherdish)*

Fornication. I see no harm in such simple homiletic teaching. They are a puritanical lot, our brothers of the north.

TARMINIUS: But, Augustine, he is doing more. He is denying Original Sin, the redemptive virtues of God's grace, even, it would seem, our salvation in Christ. He seems to be saying —that man does not need help from heaven. That man can better himself by his own efforts alone. That the City of God can be realised as the City of Man.

AUGUSTINE:

*(astounded)*

But—this—is—heresy! Oh my God—the poor lost British soul—

*There is a sudden spurt of flame which ruddies the scene. All look to its source. The camera whip-pans to the spit, where flames are fierce. A toothless scullion grins, touching a forelock in apology.*

SCULLION: Sorry, my lords, sir, gentlemen. A bit of fat in the fire.

47. GROUP SHOT

*Augustine, Tarminius, Flaccus look very grim.*

AUGUSTINE: Fat in the fire, indeed.

48. INTERIOR DAY A HOVEL

*Pelagius is talking gently and wisely to a group of poor men, artisans, layabouts, who all listen attentively. A pretty girl named Atricia sits at his feet and looks up in worship.*

PELAGIUS: In my land the weather is always gentle, rather misty, never lacking rain. The earth is fertile, and by our own efforts we are able to bring forth fair crops. The sheep munch good fat grass. There are no devilish droughts, there is no searing sun. It is no land for praying in panic—not like the arid Africa of our friend the Bishop Augustine.

ATRICIA: Oh, how I should love to see it. Could one be happy there without fear, without constant fear?

PELAGIUS: Fear of what, my dear child?

ATRICIA: Fear of having to suffer for one's happiness?

PELAGIUS: Ah yes, Atricia. In Britain we have no vision of hellfire—nor do we need to invoke heaven to make life's torments bearable. It is a gentle easy land, it is a kind of heaven in itself.

A LAYABOUT: But you said something about making a heaven there. And now you say it is a heaven already.

PELAGIUS: A *kind* of heaven I said, friend. We have many advantages. But we are not so foolish as to think we are living in the garden of Eden. No, our paradise is still to be built—a paradise of fair cities, of beauty and reason. We are free to cooperate with our neighbours, which is another way of saying *to be good*. No sense of inherited sin holds us in hopeless sloth.

ATRICIA: I can see it now—that misty island of romance. Oh, I should so love to breathe its air, smell its soil—

PELAGIUS: And why should you not, my dear? What the heart of man conceives may ever be realised. I was just saying the other day—

*There is a noise of entering feet. They all look up. They are obscured somewhat by the gross shadow of those entering.*

A VOICE (OS): Is your name Pelagius?

PELAGIUS: Why, yes—

49. PELAGIUS'S POV
*Two gross authoritative men in imperial uniform stand in the way of the sunlight. They look sternly at the assembly.*

FIRST MAN: You are to come with us. At once.

50. PELAGIUS AND ATRICIA
*She clings to him in fear. He comforts her with a patting hand.*

PELAGIUS:

(*smiling*)

You appear to be men of authority. It would be useless for me to ask why or where.

51. TWO SHOT
*The two authoritative men look at him in burly contempt.*

SECOND MAN: Quite quite useless.

52. INTERIOR DAY A CONVOCATION OF BISHOPS
*Augustine speaks while the camera pans along a line of grave bishops. Pelagius is out of shot.*

AUGUSTINE: Quite quite useless to deny that you have been spreading heresy.

53. THE SAME PELAGIUS
*Pelagius is sitting on a kind of creepystool, humble and tranquil during his episcopal investigation.*

PELAGIUS: I do not deny that I have been spreading gospel, but that it is heresy I do most emphatically deny.

54. GROUP SHOT
*A number of beetle-browed bishops beetle at him.*

AUGUSTINE (OS): Heresy—heresy—*heresy.*

55. RESUME 52.
*Augustine strides up and down the line of bishops while he speaks. His mitre frequently goes awry with the passion of his utterance, but he straightens it ever and anon.*

AUGUSTINE: Yes, sir. You deny that man was born in evil and lives in evil. That he needs God's grace before he may be good. The very cornerstone of our faith is *original sin.* That is doctrine.

56. RESUME 54.
*The bishops nod vigorously.*

BISHOPS: Originalsinriginalsinrignlsn.

57. PELAGIUS
*He gets up lithely from his creepystool.*

PELAGIUS: Man is neither good nor evil. Man is rational.

58. AUGUSTINE
*In* CU *the writhing mouth, rich-bearded, of Augustine sneers.*

AUGUSTINE: *Rational.*

59. EXTERIOR DAY A SCENE OF RIOT
*The Goths have arrived and are busily at their work of destruction. They pillage, burn, kill in sport, rape. A statue of Jesus Christ goes tumbling, breaking, pulverising itself on harmless screaming citizens. The Goths, laughing, nail an old man to a cross. Some come out of a church, bearing a holy chalice. One micturates into it. Then a pretty girl is made to drink ugh of the ugh.*

60. EXTERIOR NIGHTFALL A WINDY HILL
*Augustine and Pelagius stand together on the hill, looking grimly down.*

AUGUSTINE: Rational, eh, my son?

PELAGIUS:

(*hardly perturbed*)

It is the growing pains of history. Man will learn, man *must* learn, man *wants* to learn.

AUGUSTINE: Ah, you and your British innocence—

61. THEIR POV

*A view of the burning city. Cheers and dirty songs. Screams.*

AUGUSTINE (OS): Evil evil evil—the whole of history is written in blood. There is, believe me, much much more blood to come. The evil is only beginning to manifest itself in the history of our Christian West. Man is bad bad bad, and is damned for his badness—unless God, in his infinite mercy, grants him grace. And God foresees all, foresees the evil, foredamns, forepunishes.

62. RESUME 60.

*Augustine takes Pelagius by the shoulders and shakes him. But Pelagius gently and humorously removes the shaking hands. He laughs.*

PELAGIUS: Man is free. Free to choose. Unforeordained to go either to heaven or to hell, despite the Almighty's allfore-knowingness. Free free free.

63. THE BURNING CITY

*A vicious scene of mixed rape and torture and cannibalism. The song of a drunk is heard.*

DRUNK (OS):

(*singing*)

Free free free,
We be free to be free . . .

64. GROUP SHOT

*The drunk, surrounded by dead-drunks and genuine corpses, spills pilfered wine, singing.*

DRUNK: Free to be scotfree,
But

Not free to be not free,
Free free fr

*There is a tremendous earthquake. A tear in the shape of a Spenglerian tragic parabola lightnings across the screen.*

**AND NOW THIS IMPORTANT WORD FROM OUR SPONSOR:**

**FRSHNBKKKKGGGGRHNKSPLURTSCHGROGGLEWOK**

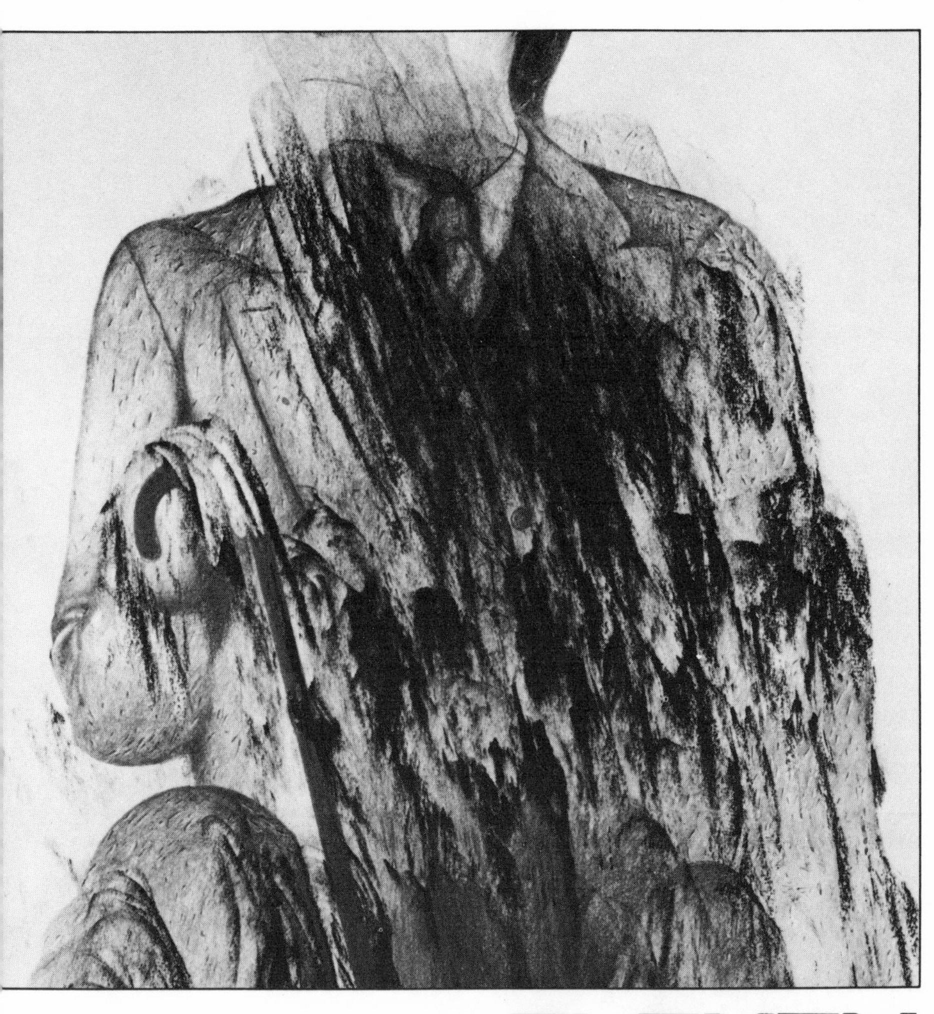

# ELEVEN

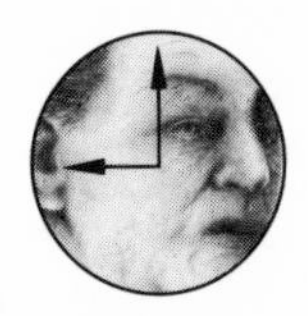

**THIS**, children, is New York. A vicious but beautiful city, totally representative of the human condition or, for any embryonic existentialists among you, *la condition humaine*. What's that when it's at home, you vulgarly ask, Felicia? You will find out, God help you, soon enough, child. It is named New York in honour of the Duke of York who became King James II of Great Britain—a foolish and bigoted monarch who tried to reimpose Catholicism on a happily Protestant nation and, as was inevitable, ignominiously failed. No, Adrian, this is no longer a British city: it is part of a great free complex or federation of states that are welded together under a most un-British constitution—rational, Frenchified, certainly republican. They revolted against the British king to whom they had once owed allegiance and tribute. No, Charles, that was a *Protestant* king and also bigoted and foolish. Let us swoop a little lower—how beautiful those exalted towers in the Manhattan dawn now we have descended to clear air under the enveloping blanket, Wilfrid. The jagged teeth of a monostomatic monster? One way of looking at it, Edwina.

We are here, under the aegis of Educational Time Trips, Inc., to seek out our poet. This is a great city for poets, though there are few like ours. We swim aerially over the island a little way, north of the midtown area, nearer to the Hudson than to the East River. He is round here somewhere. Yes, Morgana, we will have to *peek* a little. Through the dawn windows of 91st Street, as they call it (a rational city, a *numerical* city). Avert your eyes, Felicia; what they are doing is entirely their own affair. Here, dear dear, a young man is murdering his bedmate in postcoital tristity. Those two middle-aged men are actually *dancing:* it would seem somewhat early for that. A tired girl eats an insubstantial breakfast at a kitchen table. A man in undress and blue spectacles peers at the obituary page of *The New York Times*. Look at the squalor of the bedroom of that scholarly-seeming youth—cans and bottles and untidy stacks of an obviously filthy periodical. Here another murder, there a robbery, and now—the contortions in the name of pleasure, God help us.

That is interesting, that round bed. Do you see the round bed, Felicia, Andrea? Very unusual, a round bed. And on the round bed a skeletal lady sleeps alone, telling (if that tangent touches at twelve) the right time—astonishing! Eight-ten, if her lower limbs are the hour hand. But here. And now. Look look. We have found him! Gather round, children, and see. Mr. Enderby, temporary professor as we are told he is in this fashed fag end of his days, asleep naked in a nest of *pouffes*. Ugly, hairy, fat—ah yes, he always was. The television set, to which he is not listening, discourses the morning news, which is all bad. He seems, dear dear, to have been somewhat incontinent in his sleep. Gracious, the weaknesses of the great!

And now—a little surprise for you. A black woman, key in hand, of pious face but ugly gait, waddles in, sees him, is disgusted, holds up her key in pious deprecation of his besmirched nudity. But, soft. She goes closer, looks closer, touches. She holds up both her hands in expression of a quite different emotion, runs out of the room with open mouth, strange words emanating therefrom. So we now know, and it is a sort of satisfaction, for *nunc dimittis* is the sweetest of canticles. Remember us in the roads, the heaven-haven of the Reward. Let him easter in us, be a dayspring to the dimness of us, be a crimson-cresseted east. No, hardly that, I go too far perhaps. Is there anything of his own that will serve? Yes, Edmund?

> *The work ends when the work ends,*
> *Not before, and rarely after.*
> *And that explains, my foes and friends,*
> *This spiteful burst of ribald laughter.*

Stop giggling will you, all of you? You are both foolish and too clever for words, Edmund, with your stupid and irreverent and *meaningless* doggerel improvisation. You will all smile on the other sides of your faces when I get you back to civilisation. All right, all right, I am aware that I involuntarily rhymed. Come on, out of it. Another instalment of the human condition is beginning. Out of it: *he* is well out of it, you say, Andrea? But no: he is in it, we are all and always in it. Do not think that anyone can escape it merely by—I will not utter the word: it is quite irrelevant. Out of it, indeed; he is not out of it at all.

ROME, JULY 1973

## *a note on the type*

This book was set on the Linotype in Electra, a type face designed by W. A. Dwiggins. The Electra face is a simple and readable type suitable for printing books by present-day processes. It is not based on any historical model, and hence does not echo any particular time or fashion.

This book was composed and bound by
The Book Press, Inc., Brattleboro, Vermont.
Printed by The Murray Printing Company,
Forge Village, Massachusetts.
Typography and binding design by Susan Mitchell.

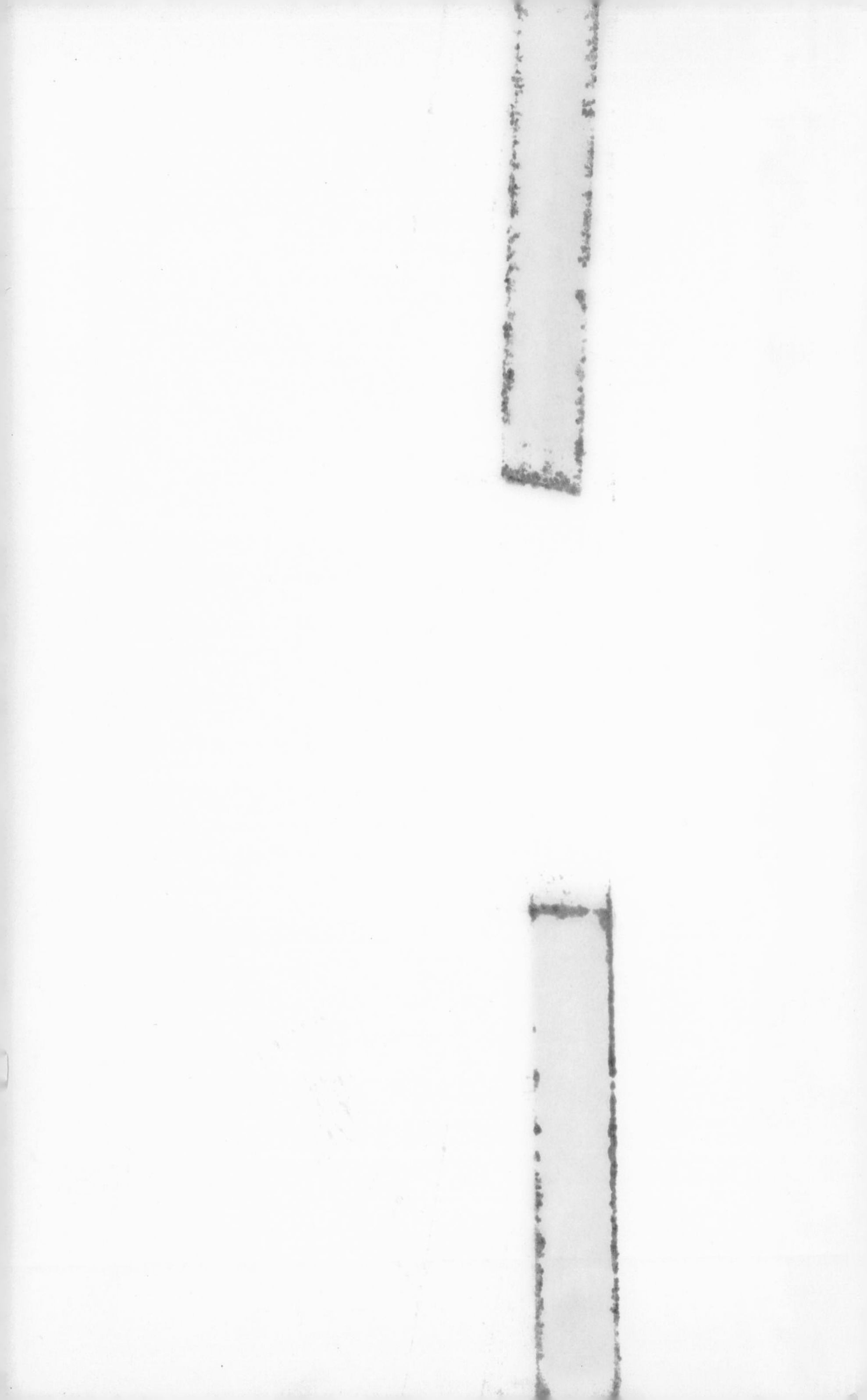